Vampire Secrets

Vampire Secrets

The Night World

KAY STELLMACH

authorHOUSE®

AuthorHouse™ LLC
1663 Liberty Drive
Bloomington, IN 47403
www.authorhouse.com
Phone: 1-800-839-8640

Published by AuthorHouse   07/10/2014

ISBN: 978-1-4969-0027-2 (sc)
ISBN: 978-1-4969-0026-5 (e)

Library of Congress Control Number: 2014905736

Chapter 1

"**I**T'S SUMMER!" My little sister Ari screamed from the dining room, hopefully playing with her Barbie dolls or something.

"Can it Ari!" I shouted back. "I'm on the phone!" I took my left hand off the speaker of the house phone. I put it back up to my ear.

"Sorry about that," I told my best friend, Riley. "My parents are making me babysit her." I groaned. "The little ray of sunshine won't stop screaming." I told her sarcastically. "Can she ever be normal?"

"That's okay, Kylie," She responded. "Luckily for me, I was blessed with being the only child." She said with a little angel voice, which sounded very unreal.

Riley was anything but an angel. You wouldn't want to see her when her parents say she can't go to the mall... it's not pretty.

"Yeah"

I got cut off by the sound of glass shattering.

"Got to go," I quickly babbled before I hung up. I stood up from the tan couch, "Ari!" I took a left out of the living room to go to the dining room. I heard her whimpering softly, and that left me wondering what the heck she just did.

Knowing her, she was probably choking on one of her Barbie's heads. Sadly, she has done that before. Not from when she was a toddler, but a week ago!

Everything looked normal though; the carpet was still white, the flower print table cloth was still one piece, and the chairs didn't have bite marks on them. All the things I've been blamed for. The little devil got caught for nothing.

She may be dumb, but the little thing is a good actress.

...And my parents aren't that bright to believe that their thirteen year old chewed their chairs, and their eight year old didn't.

C'mon people! It's called common sense!

I swear, one time they left they had told Ari to babysit me... hopefully that was just a dream. My parents wouldn't actually do that would they? Could they?

Nope, it was just a dream, I told myself after I went over all the options.

I peeked under the table. Ari was sitting under there with blood streaking her "perfect" face. And she was holding broken glass.

I put my face in my hands, that idiot!

"C'mon, let's get you cleaned up." I held out my hand to her.

"No!" She whined, but then her whining erupted into a temper tantrum. "I don't want to!" She kicked and screamed under the table.

"You got hurt, and I'm going to make you feel all better!" I fake smiled. It hurt me so badly to say that to her. I mean yes she got hurt, but now she's going to be a little brat about it!

Ari slowly crawled out from under the table, and the blood on her face started to drip onto the white carpet.

Maybe my parents won't realize there were red blotches on the white carpet? It could be a new pattern...

I examined the large cut on her forehead. "This is why you don't play with glass!" I scolded her. I grabbed her wrist and yanked her into the kitchen.

"It's not glass, its mom's vase!" Ari smiled. "You're so dumb." She started to giggle through all of her crying.

I took a deep breath. She broke mom's vase too?!

I grabbed a red washcloth and wet it, and then I started to wipe all the blood off of her face. I used a paper towel to dry it, and finally, put a big Dora the Explorer band aid on her cut. It wasn't deep, so I thought it would be enough.

"I don't like Dora though!" She whined angrily, and started to scream once again, making my ears ring.

"Too bad," I dismissed her. "Now go to your room. You're going to bed early." I gave her a shove towards the stairs.

"No!" She refused. She just stood there, giving me the puppy dog face, but trust me, I was not going to give in to her.

"Fine," I picked her up and started to walk up the stairs. "OW!"

Ari was kicking and screaming, and I just got a foot in my gut. She may be a tiny spitfire, but this girl has some hard kicks!

I took a right, and then walked down the long, wide hall down to her room. I walked across her room and firmly set her on her twin sized bed. On her nightstand was a clove of garlic. I picked it up suspiciously.

"Why do you have this?" I asked while putting it in my short's pocket. You couldn't trust this girl with anything. Not even something as simple as garlic.

"Vampires," She exclaimed. "They were on the news!"

How would she know? She doesn't even watch the news. She must be thinking of a Dora Special on the T.V.

"Ari, there are no vampires, I promise. Now go to bed." I walked out of the room, and right before I was about to shut the door, Ari started to scream again.

"It's only 9:00!" She whined. She jumped off her bed, and started to run towards me like she was a psycho killer.

"Exactly, goodnight," I shut and locked the door right before she could get to me.

She's eight. Even though it's summer, she shouldn't be staying up this late.

Phew!

I didn't want to get another foot in the gut, or have her bite me. When she gets mad or doesn't get what she wants, she bites your arm really hard. I still have lots of marks from her! That girl was an eight year old nightmare!

As soon as I locked the door, I heard the doorbell ring.

"Coming," I yelled as I ran down the stairs as fast as I could.

Geez, could I ever get a break?

I opened the large wooden door. "Hello?"

I could recognize that dark brown hair and blue eyes anywhere! It was Riley.

"Hey!" She smiled and walked into my house. Even though that was kind of rude, we were best friends, so I'd let it slide. I just don't want her doing that to random people though.

Like in fifth grade we were selling cookies for a fundraiser, and Riley would just walk straight into the person's home. She said "it helps sell the cookies because it made them feel more comfortable." But it really didn't. We were supposed to sell fifty boxes, and we only sold two. Thank you Mom and Dad.

"What are you doing here?" I wondered aloud. Not that I wasn't happy to see her, but it would be nice to know when she was coming over.

"I live a block down. I know how to walk." Riley answered in her usual edginess. "Anyway, you sounded troubled. Where's the child?"

"I put her to bed..." I trailed off. Then I noticed something different, of what wasn't there on Riley.

"Riley, where's your pants?" I asked.

I tell you, this is one interesting girl. So is Ari, but you don't see her walking around with no pants. At least she has the decency to wear them.

She pointed to the tiniest sliver of blue cloth, "This is my pants." She smiled. She tilted her head to the side a bit, wondering why I asked.

"I mean actual pants!" I joked. "We're thirteen, we don't wear," I pointed to the line of cloth. "That."

That part I wasn't joking about. We are thirteen year old girls, not thirteen year old tramps! With Riley dressing that way, it wasn't very easy to tell which one of those she was anymore.

Riley mock gasped, "How can you say that?"

"Well, it's the truth." I put my hand on my hip. I smiled a little. "Anyway, I'll be right back, I'm going to go get you some pants," I laughed a little.

If my parents saw her like this, they wouldn't be laughing. If they even knew Riley dressed like this, I would have to go find a new best friend.

"Yay," she said sarcastically, but I saw her smile too. Her gaze fell towards her pants to decide whether I was right or wrong about the whole pants switch, as I turned around to run up the white velvety stairs once again.

Man, it was becoming a workout!

It's a good thing my room was the second door upstairs. I may be athletic, but when I'm not forced to run, I'm as lazy as a sack of potatoes!

I walked over to my white dresser and opened the second drawer. I scrummaged around for a while until I found some purple shorts that were at least three inches longer then Riley's. Something caught my eye after that, though. It was a tiny red piece of paper. I picked it up and read it.

Be careful what you tell others

Be careful what you tell others?! What is this? Some sort of lame leadership club or something where we learn how to treat others?

I got nervous. That totally sounds like something my parents would do.

I dismissed the thought of my parents signing me up for a leadership club. They would tell me at least.

When I put it down, my hands had red dye or something on them. I wonder who put it there, and how they got into my house. It wasn't Ari, because the handwriting was neat.

It really creeped me out though. Who would place that in someone's room?! That gave me the feeling that I was being targeted now. I don't know, I was probably just being over dramatic.

I set it down on a small stack of paper towels so it wouldn't stain my white dresser, and then ran back downstairs.

Riley wasn't at the front door anymore though. "Riley?" I called.

I searched all over the place, the kitchen, the dining room, living room, and my dad's office. She probably didn't want the new pants, so she left.

I thought we were laughing about the pants thing. I didn't say something bad, did I? I hope not, because Riley sort of did have a short temper.

One time she didn't speak to me for a week because I accidently stole one of her shrimp puffs at a restaurant. Another time she didn't even look at me for a couple of days because we had the same crush. The only way we were still friends was because I told her I didn't like him anymore. Then she got mad at me for saying he was ugly...

Anyways, bottom line is it is hard to stay friends with her.

I yawned. I guess I'm going to go to bed now too. I was getting a bit tired from the Ari thing. After dealing with her, all I ever wanted to do was collapse in my nice, warm, welcoming bed.

Here we go, going upstairs, again.

The more I thought about it, the more I got freaked out by the note though. Perhaps Ari did do it. Right now, it was the only choice keeping me sane.

I was about to walk into my room, but I saw blood on the carpet. That's weird, seeing Ari bled on the downstairs carpet...

I must just be seeing things, I need some rest.

I ran into my room, and put my pants away in my dresser. I turned to my window because I felt a breeze. I gasped.

Except now I was going insane, my bedroom window was open! Someone had climbed through the window, and placed the note in my dresser! That means... when I was in my room, I was in it with a thief or murderer or someone!

I'm okay, don't freak out, don't freak out...

I'm freaking out!

I went over to shut it, but I saw a dark figure in the sky instead. I screamed. It looked like it had the shape of a human. I saw the shadow turn its head towards me, and it flew on, it's long straight hair following it. That was all I saw, because the figure was flying very fast.

I hopped into bed and tried to fall asleep. I also hoped that I could ignore what I had just seen. It was totally not normal.

No matter how much I tried though, I couldn't fall asleep. I finally opened my eyes once I had given up hope on sleeping. I was way too scared right now.

I shrieked. There was a person in front of me! She looked about a year or two older than me, and had light brown hair that was medium length.

She just smiled, with sharp pointy fangs! I couldn't see her all too well, besides her face, but what really stood out was her red glowing eyes!

I thought I might faint from all my fear building up. Vampires were real! She must have been the one who left the note, and the red dye... that must have been blood!

EW! I didn't even want to think about whose blood it was.

In a great blur, she ran over to the door and back in about a second. She smirked.

I remembered the garlic I confiscated from Ari! In a panicking motion, I reached into my pocket and grabbed the garlic. I didn't know what to do with it!

How was I supposed to know where to shove a clove of garlic on a vampire? Down her throat maybe?

The vampire was way too close now. Five inches away from my face, possibly? Anyways, it was not a good feeling. I built up all the courage I could to look at her mouth, which had gigantic fangs that I somehow forgot about.

How was I supposed to shove a garlic clove down her throat with those long, pointy fangs waiting to dig into my neck?

Instead, knowing I didn't have a better idea (actually I had other ideas where to shove it, but I was not that willing to go that far); I just gave her a girly slap with the garlic in my hand.

She fell over in a dramatic way.

The vampire didn't die though, she was just paralyzed. It looked like she could move her mouth by her making words.

"You don't know what you have done," The girl said, breathlessly on the floor. "Don't mess with..." She trailed off.

I bit my lip, "I think I do." I grabbed the girl's arm and dragged her slowly over to the open window. "I think it's obvious you're not wanted," I put her feet out the window, and then pushed the rest of her out the window.

THUMP! She hit the ground. I'm sure she'll be okay. She is a vampire isn't she? Anyway, I shouldn't really care. I mean, she tried to kill me, so I sort of killed her back in a way. My bedroom is on the third floor, so she just took a hard hit.

I quickly shut the window and locked it. Hopefully that will keep her out, but just in case . . . SNAP! I broke the clove in half, and then placed it in the middle of the window.

Wow, my first vampire fight lasted like, less than a minute! Plus, I won!

I still wonder what she means by "Don't mess with. . ." Who? Who shouldn't I mess with? Vampires? Don't worry, I don't want to.

Man, I was good. Now since I feel pretty safe with the garlic, I decided I was going to go to bed.

My stress melted away as I processed she was the one who left me the stupid but creepy note. Now I don't have anything to worry about for the rest of the night.

Surprisingly, I wasn't out of breath at all. Neither was the vampire though when she ran over to me so fast, probably like two hundred miles per second?

Way too fast for me to know. I barely could see her run over to me it was so fast. In my perspective, it mainly just looked like she teleported!

I hopped into bed, and pulled the covers all the way up, over my head. I may have won, but that doesn't stop the existence of vampires being real.

Knowing they could sneak up on me at any time would freak out anybody. It really doesn't help that I just had a gut feeling that not many humans survive an attack. It was just pure luck that I confiscated garlic away from Ari. . .

Ari!

I hopped out of my bed and grabbed the garlic off of my windowsill. I frantically checked around to make sure there was no vampire spying on me. It was too dark for me to realize my door was closed, so I hit it hard, and fell over.

I screamed thinking it was a vampire, because I was obviously very paranoid.

I scrambled onto my feet as quick as possible, understanding that the vampire probably shut my door so I couldn't escape as easily.

I felt for the doorknob with the hand that was empty, and finally found it. I twisted it and pulled it open in a quick motion that was very loud because I wanted to get out of my room so badly. When I opened the door I did it with so much force it hit the wall, and bounced back behind me and hit me.

I looked behind me, thinking it was a vampire again. I sighed when I saw it was just the door, but then I freaked out again when I saw the blood on the carpet again!

I wasn't hallucinating before. It might have been Ari's blood, and I didn't even understand that until now. If a vampire did try to attack her, she would be more than an easy target. First of all, she's eight and not very smart. Second of all, I took away her garlic because I thought she would wreck something with it! And third of all, I locked her in her room so she wouldn't be able to escape!

If a vampire did try to bite her, she would be a goner by now!

What kind of older sister am I?!

I rushed down the hall, and unlocked the door with a soft click. I opened the door to see Ari in the corner of her twin sized bed, crying.

I ran over to her, not sure if she had been bitten yet, and sighed relief as I saw she had no injuries other than the broken glass one.

I sat down next to her. "Ari, what's wrong?" I seethed my teeth, desperately hoping she didn't hear me screaming. If she knew I was scared, she would freak out too.

"I- I heard you screaming," she stuttered through her sobs. "Then I heard a big thump," she went on, her sobs diminishing a little.

She heard me scream, and heard a body hitting the ground. That is by no means good.

"I was only screaming because I accidently hit the door and hurt myself," I told her, not sure if that was an entire lie or not. "I'm fine now, though, so just go to sleep, everything is fine, okay?" That's where the lie came in. Everything was so not fine!

"O- Okay," her cries stopped all together. She pulled her covers up and hopped under them. I could still hear her uneasy breath.

"I'm going to go back to my room now," I kissed her head softly. She may be a little brat sometimes, but sometimes she is tolerable.

I stood up, and walked out of Ari's room back into the hallway, still clutching the garlic clove tightly. I looked into my room. It was dark, and very unwelcoming now.

I did not want to go in there. There could be something still waiting for me!

I turned around and sprinted back to Ari. I closed the door softly, and tried not to act scared in front of Ari because she had just settled down.

I went over and laid by her. "I decided that it would be best for me to stay with you. So you don't get scared," I lied. I came back to Ari because I was too scared, but hey! She didn't know that, and I wasn't planning for her to find out.

We both fell asleep in a couple of hours; once we heard our parents arrive. I did not have sweet dreams. It was just blank darkness and me feeling helpless until morning. Exactly how I felt when I was being attacked by a vampire. The feeling never went away that I was being watched that night, and it continued into the morning.

Chapter 2

"HEY MOM, I'M going to the mall!" I yelled as I opened the front door. I walked out onto the porch, and closed the door behind me. This time I wasn't freaking out, so the door didn't get angry at me and attack me like last night.

It was already 4:00 PM, so it was super-hot out. The sun felt nice on my skin because of two reasons; one, it gave me warmth, and two, I knew from myths that vampires don't come out in daylight.

It was a myth though, so let's just pray to God that it's real!

I slipped on my aviators, made sure I had my purse, and I was good! I walked down to the end of our driveway and started to wait for Riley to come pick me up.

Then I realized with my aviators, it's going to be harder for me to spot a vampire. I quickly whipped them off so I could see more clearly.

I didn't have any garlic with me, because I hoped that the sun would act as a shield. The more I thought about it, the more worried I got.

I looked around again, still having that odd urge that I was being watched. I saw a bush by the front steps move, so I backed up. When I backed up I tripped on a piece of chalk that Ari decorated the driveway with and never put away.

I fell on my butt, and that's when I realized that when the bush moved it was the wind. I still eyed the bush, making sure there was no vampire hiding in it, getting ready to pop out and suck my blood.

I had a chill run up my spine when I felt another burst of wind, and I thought it was a vampire running towards me so I stood up urgently, getting ready to run. I looked towards the street expecting a vampire to pop up magically. All I saw was a car zooming by.

Usually a normal car driving in the neighborhood wouldn't allow me to feel a gust of wind up at the top of my driveway, but this car was speeding really fast, so that freaked me out even more.

I watched the car go past, and I gave it a death stare. I just realized I hate orange Chevrolets that had a white stripe down the middle.

Never buying one of those things!

For the rest of the time until Riley showed, I just stood by my garage with my arms crossed, watching every little movement I saw. It wasn't fun waiting for Riley to come, seeing over 95% of the movements scared me. For once, I was being very impatient with Riley.

Five minutes later, Riley came, walking down the street by herself with nothing. No purse, no mom, and no mom's van.

Those five minutes really weren't worth the wait.

Honestly, now I just wanted to go into the safety of my home and barricade myself into a closet or something.

Or throw a temper tantrum like Ari, because I was really ticked off now!

"Riley, where's your mom's van?" I asked stupidly.

"Uh... whoops. I forgot to tell her." She chuckled uneasily a little. "Whatever, lets walk then, its good exercise!"

"No, because the mall is seven miles away," I rolled my eyes. "Smart..." I said sarcastically.

Just saying what person is going to the mall, and forgets her mom, and her car?! Wow, Riley is very, what's the word? Special.

"Oh yeah..." She turned around, so her back was facing me for some reason. She jolted back around quickly and blushed a little in embarrassment.

I just got that odd feeling again that I was being watched for real now, not just by the wind, but by a real person, or in this case, a real vampire.

That's when I took a good look at her. She was wearing a black off the shoulder top, with purple shorts, and let's not forget her inch thick eyeliner.

I'm really not sure why, but Riley was acting very strange. She usually didn't wear one centimeter shorts, off the shoulder tops, or makeup!

I don't know what was wrong with her, but she just seemed different. Now that I think about it, she has been acting kind of weird for the last month. She looked the same until yesterday, but now she was acting and looking really different.

"Then I guess I'll walk by myself." She told me with her edginess, and that made me feel a little bit better. But that's when she started to walk away.

"FINE, we'll walk, happy now?!" I ran to catch up with her.

I mean, she may be a different person now, but she was still my best friend. Couldn't I also tell her about vampires, since I could still tell her anything?

"Actually, yes," She pulled me behind a tree, grabbed my stomach, and then put her hand over my mouth. I also felt and saw another hand go over my eyes. What I felt next, that was super odd. It seemed like I was traveling at about two hundred miles per hour.

What was she doing? That is when I realized that the vampire encounter I had yesterday. The vampire could travel at around two hundred miles per hour!

Does that mean Riley's a vampire?!

The entire trip kind of hurt. We were going so fast, the wind was hitting my face so hard that it felt like I was having blocks of cement thrown at my face repeatedly. Bottom line, it did not feel nice.

When I could finally see again, I was in a room about as big as a master bedroom, and Riley was nowhere in sight.

Not only is she a vampire and never told me, she abandoned me in a place where I have no idea in the least where it was.

It had red walls, black carpet, and a single chair in the middle. Even thought it was lacking furniture, it still looked very fancy.

There were also these creepy guys with fangs and red eyes guarding the door. One was kind of short, but he was still very intimidating, and the other one was already intimidating because he was tall and had lots of muscles.

All of the sudden, a strong shove made me fall into the chair. I banged my knee on it, but I still fell into the chair.

I felt a gashing pain, but I didn't say anything because I doubt anybody would care. I mean, Riley is my best friend, and she wouldn't even care!

I looked the way it came from, and it was a girl with long, wavy, blonde hair. She also had red eyes and fangs. She looked about twenty years old.

"Well look what we have here, a human who knows the existence of vampires." The girl spoke with a soft voice, but it was stern at the same time. "Well I guess that's what you get when you send a newbie." She scoffed, and crossed her arms.

She may be like, one hundred, but she still had the attitude of a teenager.

"What are you talking about?" I wondered aloud, knowing I probably won't get an answer.

To my surprise though, I did. "When you become a vampire, and you want a good name in the vampire world, you start at the bottom- as a newbie. With you, you start at the middle. Do you know how many people have actually survived a vampire attack?" The girl actually sounded sort of nice now.

"Um... Five?" I randomly guessed.

"Two, including you, the other girl eventually got bitten, her name was Faith." She rambled on...

"Who's that?" I questioned, participating in the history lesson.

"Me," Faith told me. "And now for that, I've been the vampire ruler for the US for about seventy years now." She bragged. "Well, anyways, I brought you here because I need you to do me a favor." Faith walked towards me, and gave me a little smirk. That told me, it was not going to be fun.

"What is it?" I cringed, thinking of all the things she would send me to do. Including, fighting a better more advanced vampire this time, and probably die!

"First of all, tell no one of vampires, and second, the most important favor is; go into Clutch Woods tonight. You are to find…" She looked around the room. "An orange and blue leaf," She said unsurely. She gave me a funny look, it sort of made me feel like she was trying to make me seem stupid or something.

"Uh, okay." Something in her voice made me unsure of what I was looking for, or if I was even was looking for something at all. Inside of me, I felt like this was a trap. Now, it was just up to me to decide if I'm going to go into Clutch Woods tonight or not.

Plus, that seems like an unrealistic task. She wants me to find an orange and blue leaf in a huge forest at night when it's summer?

"And if you don't do it… then you can guess what's going to happen next…" Faith trailed off.

She looked at one of the guards with wide eyes, as if they were reading each other's minds. This was the less buff guard, who had the new Justin Bieber hair.

"Don't worry, I get it," I stood up, ignoring the odd moment between a ruler and one of her guards, if that was even a thing. "Now have one of your goons bring me home." I demanded.

She gave a hint of a smile. "And you already know how stuff goes down around here."

Gosh, can she knock it off with the creepy smiles?!

I rolled my eyes, "it would be impossible for me not too." I looked at Faith, the only thing I saw in her was being a bossy brat.

"Now," she said, "which one of my goons do you want to bring you home?"

"I don't care!" I yelled. It's not like I'm going to go through a long list of names and photos deciding which one will take me home!

Faith snapped her paper white fingers and Riley appeared in a blur.

I gasped, Riley is a vampire! That settles it; I no longer had a best friend!

"Riley, bring this little kiddie home." Faith ordered, losing all the niceness in her voice. Faith crossed her arms and stared at Riley with cold, hard eyes.

And that was a BIG mistake. I do not trust this girl, no matter what. That look that she was giving me, I bet it was to see if I actually believed her. Under that creepy smile of hers, was a big huge heaping pile of lies.

I am not going to be her suck up, even if my life depended on it, but in my situation, it sort of does. If she bites me, then that just gives me a chance to fight back. So either way, she loses.

Riley gave a silent nod, and came over to me. "Sorry," she whispered. Her voice sounded pained, which made me forgive her for a second. Then I blinked back to reality.

Oh, and I'm not even going to get started on Riley. After all the times when she could have said sorry, there wasn't a worse moment when she could have apologized then now.

"Don't cover my eyes this time. I sort of want to make sure that my ex-best friend doesn't throw me off a cliff." I replied, using her edginess against her. It felt better on this side of it.

Faith gave another one of her famous creepy smiles. Just pointing out, those smiles make super bad first impressions.

"Does that mean you were planning to have Riley actually throw me off a cliff?!" I screamed.

Faith frowned, "no." She tapped her foot once on the ground. "Do you actually think I would send a child to throw another child off a cliff?"

Yes. "No," I lied. "Because you seem to be very... um... pretty and nice for a vampire..." I was just throwing out words now. I couldn't stand the fact I was sucking up to her!

"Why thank you," Faith smiled one of her not creepy smiles finally. The first real emotion she has showed me so far.

Riley put one of her hands on my arms. She put on a firm grip to show me that she really didn't mean to bring me here, and that she wasn't planning to hurt me. I'm not sure I believed her though, considering she has lied to me so much!

Even though I still hated Riley, this showed that she didn't hate me. That may be the best news I've gotten all day! Who am I kidding, it was.

"Well, what are you doing just standing there, Ryland?" Faith ordered rudely, also saying it a little bit louder then it needed to be.

Riley cleared her throat, "It's Riley, and just so you know, I'm done doing your dirty work! In case you're wondering, I really don't care if I don't get a good name in the vampire world anymore, because there are more important things out there." Riley stood up to Faith.

Riley tightened her grip on my arm, and put her hand over my eyes again. That's when I started to feel the wind crashing down on me again.

"Thanks for covering my eyes again," I said sarcastically.

"Trust me; you'll like your eyes closed while doing this over having them wide open." Her voice sounded sincere.

Even though I still didn't think we were best friends again, her voice promised I could trust that statement. And who knows, maybe I'll be doing this with my eyes wide open one day.

Chapter 3

O   KAY... FINISHED! I had garlic lining the door and window to
     make sure that Faith doesn't send any of her wannabes after
me. That girl definitely let the power go to her head.

It was 10:00 PM and I finally felt like I could go to bed without
worries.

I slipped into bed with my frog shorts and my pajama button up
tank top. I pulled up the covers, feeling a bit of regret, of what has
happened today. Maybe I should have gone into Clutch Woods, not
to find the stupid leaf, but to see what Faith was really up to.

I had just remembered that my parents weren't home though.
That didn't really make me feel good, but at the same time I wasn't
feeling that good anyways. The only good thing is that they sent
Ari off to a sleepover.

It is really helping not to have Ari here. If she ever found out
about vampires, it will be the end for all of us. She would never shut
up about it, ever!

I closed my eyes and tried to relax. All that came to my mind
though was me being a vampire, pale skin, sharp teeth, red eyes, and
sucking human blood.

I mean, seriously?! That's disgusting! Plus vampires age so
slowly. I don't want to be thirteen for like, a hundred years!

I finally realized that my "relaxing" wasn't working. I opened my eyes and sat up straight.

I screamed as loud as I could, for the second time in two days. In front of me was another girl who looked about twenty. She had long, black, wavy hair like me. But of course I don't have fangs and red eyes.

The smirk faded quickly, though. The girl looked slightly baffled now, but then shook it off quickly. "Oh look, I don't need to lock the door because you already did it for me." The girl said with a touch of rudeness. She ran over to me in a blur. "Everyone listens to Faith." She whispered when she was about an inch away from me. Seriously, stop being creepy, and get out of my personal bubble!

I shook off my fear. I should have known this was going to happen anyways. So I thought while having the worst moment of my life, I could add a little pizazz to it.

"Well, obviously everybody except me," I smirked. "Remember? I'm special, I survived a vampire attack." I stated like I was the most important person in the world. That means I was acting like this one girl in my grade, Zoey Coleman!

The vampire gave me a mean look. "Apparently that's not the only way your special. You're not too bright kid." She told me, while her red eyes stared at me intently; searching everything on me, like she thought I had something important.

"Who are you calling a kid?! Come on, you are barely an adult!" I shot back. "You should really learn what to say at the right time." I rolled my eyes, still carrying on the snobby voice.

I could tell I was irritating her because she was getting angrier.

"You better watch what you say," she threatened. She pinned me to my bed, "'Cause it could make your life even worse."

"Come on, is that the best you can do?" I challenged. I kicked up my legs and pushed as hard as I could on her stomach. The vampire fell back a couple steps. I used that time to run over to my window, and grabbed two garlic cloves.

"Oh crud," she groaned. She put her arms halfway up, showing defeat. That kind of surprised me.

Oh wait; this might be the best moment of my life!

"Wait a minute," she held up her pointer finger, "a vampire hunter?"

"I'm not a vampire hunter," I looked down. "I guess I am now," I smirked evilly, and looked back up at her, even though I was supposed to be the good guy.

The vampire looked scared of me now. "What do you want from us?"

"You guys out of my life," I got closer.

"This is the part where I'm supposed to run, right?" She wondered aloud, looking at the window like it was her best friend, which in this case, it probably was.

I walked over to the window and opened it. "Go for it," I told her while pointing at the window. "Bye now, whatever your name is."

"Amara!" She yelled as she flew out the window.

I crossed my arms and leaned on the wall. Hey, maybe good things did happen when you used Riley's edginess!

Ha, that better teach them not to mess with me. I think I'm going to teach them who is boss for sure. Watch out, things just got worse for the vampire society.

Now for real I felt I could relax for the first couple of days. I hopped in bed, still clutching the garlic cloves.

Something still didn't add up, and I couldn't figure out what. Just something seemed a bit strange about Amara. Honestly, I think when she "fell back" it was fake. It was just a gut feeling I had. I don't know, I'm probably wrong, but I still won't let that part go yet.

I rolled over in my bed, and slowly drifted off.

The next day I was outside, sitting on the front steps. I was staring at the ground, thinking about everything that has happened so far. Nothing made sense, but of course I was talking about a fantasy creature here!

I heard the door behind me open, but I just ignored it, and kept staring at the ground. I really hoped it wasn't Ari, secretly though, because the little jerk would probably dump cold water on my head.

"Kylie, honey, what's wrong?" Mom sat next to me, and wrapped her long arms around me tightly.

I looked up at her, "Huh, nothing, nothing at all!" I scooted over a bit from her, making her frown. Come on! Can't a thirteen year old girl just go about things by herself? And... If Mom ever found out I was involved with vampires, she would most likely send me to a weird 24 hour mental hospital for the rest of my life!

She gave me that look, that was trying to make me tell her, but I had to refuse it. I mean what was I supposed to say? "Oh yeah Mom, I've been dealing with vampires for the past couple days, can you give me some advice?" How is she going to respond to that? She'll think I'm a nutcase for sure, which will give her no better place than to send me away.

She didn't wipe the look off of her face, and I started to think that she might get stuck that way. I stood up this time, "I'm going to Riley's!" I blurted, not thinking at all. Out of everything I could have said, I chose that one! I would have to preferred to say, "Oh yeah mom, I'm going to go vandalize the alley by the mall." Even that would be better!

Mom put her shoulder length blonde hair behind one ear. "Uh, okay, does she know you're coming over?" She stood up too.

Not like she deserves to know, "Um yeah sure!" I smiled, and ran off as fast as I could, which frankly, was very slow. I could never run fast to begin with. After I thought I was out of sight, I started to walk. After all, Riley's house was only like a block away.

I guess having this chance to talk to Riley was okay. I mean, we would eventually have to make amends if she still wanted to gain my trust back.

Once I reached her big, brown house, I walked up the light cement driveway, and straight up to her door. I rang her doorbell, and there was no answer. Then, I heard faint talking from the back of her house.

I snuck to the back, peeking around the corner. I saw Riley, Faith, and Amara. They were all huddled under a large oak tree in Riley's huge backyard.

Good luck to try getting my trust back now!

"...That should keep her fooled for a bit, don't you think? That was some good acting Riley! I think you totally played her!" Faith patted Riley on the back. "Do you think you could get her at my house at midnight?"

"I'm not sure, but thanks." Riley smiled. "When are we going to bite her?" She asked them. She paced around for a minute.

"Hold it!" Amara shouted. "I smell that little rat!" They looked around. "I got left," she immediately told them.

"I got right," Riley said, and she walked to the right side of her house, and Amara started walking left, towards me.

I looked at my hands, I was empty handed! How was I supposed to beat three vampires that were like five times stronger and faster than me, if I had nothing to fight with? At this moment, I really would have preferred to be vandalizing an alley by the mall!

Amara spotted me. "Found her!" She yelled. Faith and Riley instantly blurred to her sides, with all of them giving me a cold glare.

I gasped in amazement.

"You can beat one, how 'bout three?" Amara smirked. She walked closer to me, and popped out her fangs.

Yep! I was wrong! I did imagine it. Amara did not go easy on me the night before, and she wasn't planning to now.

"I don't know..." I looked down. "I'm not sure I can surrender to three idiots." I gave a fake frown. I sat down on the ground, and looked up at them, hoping somehow, I could trick them in an odd way I was making up as it went on.

"What in the world are you doing?!" Faith asked, and eyed me suspiciously. She too now, was walking towards me slowly.

"I'm surrendering to three idiots..." I lay down on my back, still staring at the three. "Do whatever you want to me. I don't care." I said quietly.

"Uh... okay." Faith smiled. She Bent down beside to me, and popped out her fangs. She faked jolted her head towards my neck, acting like she was going to bite me. I think she was expecting me to flinch, but I didn't. I noticed the gleam in her eyes that she was toying with me.

"Just make it quick..." I hinted a smile.

Faith scoffed, "I wish I could. Frankly kid, you got lucky vampires can't kill during daylight. It's too worth the risk of exposing our secret."

Wow! Improvising that I knew what I was doing paid off quite a lot! It gave me at least another ten hours of being human, and I was actually very happy about that.

"But that just means you're getting it twice as worse tonight," Faith gave me yet another one of her famous smiles.

I gave a fake pained face, and sat up. "Aw, but you forget I still have garlic at home!" I stared at Faith, who was still bending down next to me.

She stood up, having her back towards me. It kind of gave me an idea what her personality was towards vampires, just by the back of her shirt. It was red lace, which started about halfway up her back, leaving the upper half left open. "Or do you?" She turned towards me again.

At first I didn't get it, but about thirty seconds later all the color drained from my face. "How did you get into my house, and actually touch the garlic without getting paralyzed?"

Faith looked at me like I was dumb, "I thought you already put the puzzle pieces together to discover Amara was only a decoy." She put her hands on her hip. "I guess you didn't know either that I have some human servants, that I had grab the garlic for me." She got really close to me; maybe three inches away from me, so I felt every breath she took. "It's too bad you still had garlic in your room, so Amara couldn't take you back to my headquarters so you could join the other few humans we had working there."

I could feel my heart pulse quickening, with every moment. "Wait! I still have the garlic in my room!" I exclaimed. "Ha!"

She shook her head, "your mom thought differently. Let's just say after she put it in the outside garbage, I did the honors myself to transport it to the dump."

I stumbled back a few steps.

"Yep, Kylie, you really thought you had the upper hand, miss vampire hunter," Amara sneered. "Also about that whole vampire hunter thing, I think it's killed and done. Your whole campaign lasted about ten hours, without one vampire attack. So you probably should have done it when you actually had the supplies."

They were all right, I was powerless. They had the upper hand now, and could end my life in a second. Now, I knew for sure, anytime at night I could wake up to a new life.

"Well," Faith smirked. "See you tonight." And they all flew off, including Riley, who never said anything throughout the chat.

Chapter 4

I WAS WALKING BACK to my house, thinking about the talk I just had with Faith and Amara, trying to think of any loose ends I could find, so that I had the upper hand. I thought about everything, not finding one small place I could slip into so I wouldn't become a vampire.

I thought about going to the store to buy a bunch of garlic, but that idea got shot down pretty quickly. First of all, I would have to pay for a bunch of garlic with my own money, and I was broke. Second of all, my parents would have to bring me, and they both are at a conference for their work. And third, everyone would question why I had bought so many garlic cloves.

I walked up to my house, realizing that I would have to babysit Ari again. Wow! This day was just getting better and better!

I walked through the front door, to see my mom pacing around, with my dad as well. "Good your home! Bye now!" My mom shouted, and ran out of the door wearing the ugliest pink heels I've ever seen in my thirteen years of life.

Ari peaked from behind a corner, and then realized they had left. She jumped out from behind it, and immediately started the demands. "I'll take a grilled cheese sandwich with an ice cold glass of lemonade, NOW."

I looked at her blankly, "now, why in the world would I do that for you?" I put my hand on my hip and stared her down.

She gave me a bright smile, "because I know that you broke mom's vase."

I groaned Ari could get away with anything, because she always blamed it on me! I rolled my eyes, "Coming up princess."

I walked over to the kitchen and started to cook the sandwich, still watching her as best as I could to make sure she didn't do something else stupid. I was watching her like a hawk, until she disappeared up the stairs.

"Hey! Where do you think you're going?!" I shouted after her, but knowing her sparkling wit, she only started to scream and run away.

I rolled my eyes, could I ever have it easy?!

I looked back at the grilled cheese I was making, and it was half finished already. I turned off the stove, dumped it on a black plate, and yelled.

"Ari, you're coming back down if you want food, one... two... three..." I started to count. I heard footsteps as Ari made a mad dash for the kitchen.

I poured her a glass of lemonade and set it down by the grilled cheese. "Eat up," I looked at her expectantly.

She ate it quickly, and ran away to the living room to play with her dolls.

I looked at the clock. Three more hours until Ari goes to her sleepover. And the time did not go by fast...

I sighed in relief as Ari's friend Lila picked her up, leaving me home alone. I didn't like being home alone with all that had been happening, but it was better than taking care of Ari plus all the added stress from the vampires.

I walked up to my room as I usually would, except knowing the weight on my shoulders that this was going to be my last night human. It was only 9:00 PM, but I wanted to sleep a little until my life turned upside down. To my disappointment though, no matter how many times I rolled over and tried to get comfortable, I never did.

Finally, a couple hours later I just gave up. I sat up straight, and looked around my room; still no vampire in sight. I stood up, and got startled by a rattling of a nearby chime. Even though the sound was high pitched, it felt low and ominous, as if I were in a horror movie!

Suddenly, I felt breathing on my neck and turned around to see a vampire behind me. He had big red eyes, but I couldn't tell anything else from the darkness. I turned back around, to face Amara, who was carrying on the tradition of Faith's creepy smiles.

I started to run, but they were obviously faster. They were in front of me, slowly getting closer. THUMP! I tripped over a book I had lying in my bedroom, and was now on the ground cornered. For once, I wished Ari was here. I wished my parents were here. Anybody human would be nice.

Amara dived onto me, sinking her perfect sharp fangs into my neck. I started to scream, but it was no use. Every second the pain got worse, and Amara showed absolutely no mercy, keeping her fangs sealed on my neck, sucking the life out of me. Finally, everything went black, and I couldn't feel anything anymore. Not even the vicious pain that made my neck throb.

I woke up in my room, in my bed. My alarm was beeping very loudly; I hit the button to shut it up. I glanced at the time, 8:30 AM!

I totally forgot my parents put me on a schedule to wake up at 8:30 every morning in the summer, to practice for school! Of course my parents weren't up yet, they set their alarm for 10:30 AM every day! It was totally ridiculous!

That's when I realized what had happened this past night. I jumped out of bed and looked in my dresser mirror. I still had a reflection, so that was good!

Huh, must have had a nightmare! I surely couldn't be a vampire. I only looked a little pale in the mirror, but that didn't matter. I checked my neck, it was a bit red, but I must have slept on it wrong. It didn't hurt at all, like in my nightmare, so it surely couldn't have been real.

The only obvious reason is that I was still human. I mean, I didn't even have fangs! What type of vampire doesn't have fangs exactly?

None! All vampires have fangs, so I was safe. No vampire here!

I rubbed my eyes wearily, while opening my door, and walking downstairs quietly. Once I reached the kitchen, I dug through the cupboard hungrily. I grabbed my favorite cereal, Nutty Honey Loops. The perfect combo of dry cereal and honey!

Yeah, I have no idea why it's my favorite cereal.

I shook it making sure there was enough for me. Ari had a bad habit of pouring a big bowl of it, eating a few bites, and throwing the rest away. She had a bad personality in every possible way!

It felt at least half-way full, so that was good.

I pulled the fridge door open, and grabbed the gallon bottle of skim milk. I took the shiny yellow bowl in the lower cupboards, and mixed the cereal and milk in the bowl. For some odd reason, just the look of it didn't make me as excited as I usually am when I am about to eat it.

Well, usually to me it just looks like dried out sugar, so I guess it wasn't really a difference, but still, it didn't have that usual appeal it gives me. Something just wasn't... right. I had no idea what it was, but I had a gut feeling it wasn't good.

I sat down at our light brown rectangle table, and shoved a big scoop of milk and Honey Loops in my mouth. It didn't taste as good as it used too, and that confused me seeing even if I'm not in the mood to eat it, it still tastes great! I'm pale, food doesn't taste very good... I must be getting sick!

I went over to my family's medicine cabinet, and grabbed a thermometer. I stuck it under my tongue, and waited for a couple minutes. It started to produce a light beeping, but it sounded very loud to me. I took the thermometer out of my mouth, and read it. It said 32 degrees Celsius!

Um, usually when it goes down it goes down to maybe 95 degrees lowest. Not 32, though! What was happening?!

I read it over and over, and my vision got clearer looking at it every time. I finally put it down, and walked away from it.

Oddly, I smelt something really good from the kitchen, and it smelt like it was coming from the dining room. I ran to the dining room to check it out, and I was attracted to the carpet. The red part of the carpet, which was Ari's stained blood!

Okay, this is getting out of hand! I cannot be a vampire! All signs are pointing to it though! Then the answer struck me. There was only one way to find out. Vampires can heal really fast, right?

With that, I fast walked to the kitchen again, and grabbed a steak knife. I pointed the sharp side to my wrist, and I cut it slightly.

A tiny river of blood came flowing out of it, like it usually would if a normal teenager girl cut herself. I looked at it closely, trying to find anything suspicious. I thought it would instantly heal, but I was wrong. So as fast as I could- this was not that fast since I was a very lazy person- I washed the blood off the knife, and my wrist to make sure no one knew I cut myself. If my mom found out, she would definitely take me to a therapist!

Then I scoffed. She had every right to. I was thirteen, and I thought the existence of vampires was real, and I was questioning if I was one! I'm already halfway to the loony bin here! Kidding, I happen to be there already!

Wait a minute, I had one more test to prove I wasn't a vampire! As I have seen, vampires can fly and run super-fast. Me, well I'm the complete opposite! I run slower than a turtle!

Actually I'm slower than my Grandma, because have you ever seen the woman go to her couch in less than ten minutes?!

I jumped in the air trying to fly, but of course, I didn't. Next, I ran as fast as I could through the long, narrow hallway connecting the kitchen and living room. I ran a bit faster than normal, but that was most likely from my good night's sleep.

I smiled broadly, that all just proved I wasn't a vampire! Maybe I didn't have to go to a mental facility! I ran upstairs to my room, and threw on a dark purple top, white shorts, and black flats. Since my parents were still asleep, I thought I could take a quick walk down the street. I know that's when all the bad things happen, but I didn't care. My world was filled with happiness right now, and knowing what has happened over the days, I only had one reason to be happy and that was that I wasn't a bloodsucking beast who never sleeps! I was a healthy- not nutty- thirteen year old girl! I had something HUGE to be happy about!

I walked out of the door, feeling the summer heat of Verona Park on my skin. It felt nice, seeing I've had the shivers for the past couple of days. I walked down to the end of my driveway, and gasped.

In front of me was Amara, with her arms crossed. "Enjoying life?"

I rolled my eyes and ran down my steep driveway to her. "Amara, what do you want? Just leave me alone already!"

My gosh, will this girl ever quit it? Just so you know, when you're nineteen, stalking thirteen year olds isn't a good hobby!

"I was just wondering how this morning was. Feel anything... new?" Amara walked closer, as she obviously had some of Faith rub off on her. If anything, Amara was almost creepier!

"Nope," I lied. "Everything is perfectly great!" I told her through gritted teeth.

"I didn't know you would like being a vampire so much," she smirked as she noticed I didn't realize it actually happened.

I bit my lip, "I had it coming," I said in a quiet voice. No wonder I was a vampire! Human food doesn't taste very good, my temperature is 32 degrees, and I was attracted to my little sister's stained blood on the carpet! Why did I keep lying to myself?

Amara gave me a smile, but it never reached her eyes. "No kidding you had it coming! You better not bring in anybody else on your little secret now, or the same thing will happen to them!" Amara threatened me with a hard voice, and the smile on her lips disappeared.

I backed up a little, "you don't have to tell me twice!"

"I better not!" She barked at me harshly.

Honestly, what was I thinking when I thought Amara was holding back? If this is her holding back, I don't want to see her when she's going all out!

"Listen," my voice wavered and I lost all confidence. "I don't want any trouble, okay? Just leave me alone, and I'll leave you alone."

"I would like nothing to do with you, but frankly I have to. You don't seem like you have that edge and agile that a vampire needs to have, so I need to assign someone to whip you into shape." Amara gave me a disgusted look, and I wanted to give it right back to her, but sadly I still knew she had the upper hand in this situation.

"Hey, I'm not out of shape!" I yelled at her. "I'm just not always in a rush to do things," I shot back. "I did gymnastics and karate!"

"How long?" Amara scoffed at me.

"Five years karate, three years gymnastics," I said not knowing whether that was a good answer, or bad one.

Amara used her super strength to push me down, and had her single foot pin me to the ground. The bad part is that she didn't even try to do it softly.

"Ow!" I moaned as I felt the smashing pain on my back.

"Listen kid, when you're a vampire, none of that matters. So those five years were a waste out of your next thousand years living." Amara looked at her nails, pretending to be more interested in them than me. "So I would stop saying that to impress people."

Man, this girl was a self-esteem booster for sure! As if.

"Okay," I tried to say as loud as I could, but that is kind of hard when you can't get much air because there's a vampire crushing your lungs. "Just tell me who you're going to assign me to make me act more vampire-ish." I spit out as fast as I could.

"How about your BFF?" She said in a mocking tone. "Riley is it?"

Seriously it's not cool to stalk and torture thirteen year old girls! Can Amara just get over herself and move on to twenty year old guys who won't find it creepy?

She took off her foot and stared me down. "Hey rainbows, meet Riley at her house at 12:00 A.M. tonight, she'll teach you the basics. That may take a while though."

"Too bad, my parents will never let me out that late!" I sat up and smirked. "Sucks for you, Amara, for once you won't get your way!"

Amara burst out laughing. "See what I mean? You don't need permission from your mommy, you sneak out! It's what vampires do!"

She does realize she is probably a hundred years old, and she acts like a jerky teenager! Believe me; I think she wasted all those years trying to act "hip."

"So, I better go, I have more important things than you." She pushed off of the ground as hard as she could it looked like, and in a huge burst of wind, she shot up into the sky like a rocket.

I stood up, and watched the blur move so fast, soon, I couldn't even recognize it. I knew it was a vampire power, and I was totally against vampires, but I couldn't help wondering one thing. When would I be able to do that?

Chapter 5

I T WAS 11:50 PM, and I was franticly pacing around my room. I was seriously supposed to sneak out? I've never done that!

I looked at my image in the mirror. It looked as if I was a ghost, because I was almost see-through, but I could still see what I looked like. I had put my hair into a high pony tail, so I could easily move. It didn't help how my bangs kept falling onto my face though. I wore a dark purple shirt and black shorts to kind of blend in with the vampire crowd in a way.

To be honest, I knew Amara was right. I wasn't the vampire type. If I just pretend for a night, maybe they will leave me alone for once. It didn't seem like other vampires had severe issues with the council like I did. I really just needed them to loosen the ropes on me.

I stopped pacing as I remembered my wrist. I looked down at it suddenly, and felt over the backside of my wrist to see if the cut had healed. When I saw that it did, I just had to accept the cold hard facts that I had to make this new life work.

I guess it is good that if I get hurt my injury will be quickly healed, but I really just wasn't ready for this.

Ugh! I finally had to except that this was my life now for real! I needed to sneak out. Even if I went into denial, it still wouldn't change what I was.

I opened my window slowly, trying to make no noise. I pushed the screen out. I leaned over to see the screen topple down and hit the ground. I looked in front of me, getting set to take flight.

Wait a minute, what the heck was I doing?! I couldn't fly! My room was on the third level of our house, and I expected myself to jump out?!

Uh, no, no way is that happening! I closed my window, but I didn't lock it for some strange reason.

Instead, I walked out the door of my room. Running down the stairs as fast as I possibly could, that's when I realized I must have been running 50 some miles per hour! Not as fast as the other vampires, but it would do to run to Riley's.

I couldn't do it that well though. I ended up slamming into the door, and made a loud thump! I fell to the ground, and clung to it for a moment.

After lying on the ground for a moment, I wearily hopped up as I remembered I'd be dead meat if my parents EVER saw me sneak out!

I picked myself up, and opened the door as quietly as possible, but when I opened the door, it made a big creaking noise, as it usually does.

Why now, out of all times, is when I have to act like a complete idiot?

After I finally made it out of the house of doom, I started to run to Riley's as fast as I could. It was kind of feeling the nice cool wind outside. Inside I felt hot and tense. But maybe that was because I was sneaking out for the first time in my life.

This time, I had a little bit easier time of stopping at 50 miles per hour. This time I didn't run into a door, I ran into a small tree! It still hurt, but now I was healing much faster. I could probably heal my wounds in like a minute now!

I stood up again, and when I looked straight again, I almost screamed. Riley was in front of me, smiling to herself.

I sniffed for a moment. I could actually smell Riley. She kind of had her own smell, one that stuck in my brain for good. This is one thing I had never experienced before, is that she smelt like me. Like a... vampire maybe?

"Hey, don't laugh at me, I bet you had a hard time at first too!" I scolded Riley, while she walked even closer to me.

"Let's go," she said coolly while crossing her arms, making me get that kind of feeling that Amara gave me earlier.

"How, I can't fly?" I asked her. Wow. Riley was still Riley inside. Not too bright.

"You actually can," she told me. "Actually most newbies have a very hard time learning how to fly, but hopefully that's not the case with you." She gave me a dead-to-me look with her pale white face.

"Well maybe it won't if you teach me." I looked at her with hopeful eyes, while trying to be sarcastic, but this time it didn't really work because I was so eager to get this done with. "I mean, I can already run pretty fast," I pointed out.

"Wait a second..." Riley looked around like she was looking for someone. "How fast can you run?" This time, the expression was interested, like it was some big deal.

"I don't know, like 50 miles per," I admitted to Riley.

Suddenly, I smelt something like Riley, I didn't know what smell it was exactly, but it was a normal smell, like there was a person nearby like me, which there was, aka Riley. It kind of smelt like there was three times that though. I looked around now, looking for the site of the source. One thing I could tell for sure is that it was a vampire, because of the first scent Riley gave me.

I ran around to a big, fat oak tree that was next to Riley's big house. There, all I felt was a strong burst of wind, like a vampire or two had just flown away. Was a vampire really there, or was I imagining it?

I took it as a fragment of my imagination, because I have been acting so nutty lately. I ran back to Riley in a slow stride.

I could tell that she was trying to pretend like that didn't happen. "So anyways... To fly you are on the ground, and then you kind of just push off." Riley stated while showing me how she did it.

I did exactly what she did, and it a matter of seconds I was floating in the air! Hey, that was actually pretty easy!

I turned my head over to Riley, who had her mouth open in pure shock. "It usually doesn't ever happen this fast," After she said that, her shock turned into a smile. "C'mon, Kylie, let's go," and she zoomed slowly in the air, waiting for me to catch up.

Instead of me going as slow as her, I zoomed right past her going super-fast. Finally I stopped to wait for Riley to catch up.

"Okay, so what house do you want to pick?" She pointed to the houses under us.

Which house do I want? It's not like I plan who I want to suck the blood out of, although it would be nice if I had to get revenge.

"How about this one," I pointed to a big brick house with a short driveway. That must be one of those Lakeshore houses. Lakeshore always was the home to the rich people in our neighborhood. For this case, the rich people weren't very nice, which reminded me that Riley lived in Lakeshore, so the puzzle pieces fit together now don't they?

"Perfect," Riley smirked. We both flew down there, and landed on the ground hard, since I didn't know how to land soft yet. Riley didn't mention anything, so inferred that you can't exactly teach it to newbies, or Riley is insanely lazy and rude. I was going with lazy and rude.

"Now," She pointed with her almost paper white arm at the window, "open the window." She commanded.

Following her orders since I knew I had no way out of this, I flew up to the window with ease and pulled at hard as I could. I smiled after I opened the window with my bare hands.

I had to admit, I was tempted to drop to the ground and flex my arms and say, "look at these guns!"

Also, for a while; I forgot that I had snuck out of my house because I had so much on my mind. I know what you're thinking; how can I have so much on my mind when I'm a vampire, about to suck blood, when that is the definition of what vampires do? I was a vampire physically, but mentally, I was still part human.

"Now go in there and eat," Riley instructed.

Now the fun came! I had to drink human blood! To me, that was like being a cannibal, and how utterly gross is that?

I knew inside that I really had to do this since that was practically my only source of energy. Human food doesn't taste very good anymore.

I took a big jump into the room, and saw a girl about the age of fourteen, sleeping in a queen sized bed. She had blonde hair, hazel eyes, and was wearing a purple nighty.

I ran over to the door, shut it and locked it in a matter of three seconds. I did it so quietly that the girl was still sleeping soundly! So I ran over to her, shook her hardly, and ran back to the other side of her large bedroom.

The girl woke up with fear in her eyes, and sat up straight. She looked around quickly, and she gasped when she saw me, leaning against her wall, with my arms crossed.

I looked confident and totally not freaked out in my appearance, but I was actually screaming in my head. Wow. I just realized how deceiving my looks were.

"Who-who are you?" She shivered with fear. By now she was standing up, walking towards me with a baseball bat, that she had by her bed.

I tried to smirk and look intimidating, "Do you really think that baseball bat scares me?" As I asked her that, she swung it towards me, thinking she would hit me in the stomach, but I ran to the side to avoid it. I still ran into her door though.

Not as hard as last time though, so I was getting better at running! That's probably the only good thing coming out of this. I turned towards her again, and now she had dropped the baseball bat in awe.

"How did you do that?!" She questioned, with her jaw dropped wide open in fear.

I walked towards her, cornering her. Could I really do this?!

I was just about to bite her when I remembered; I don't know how to pop out my fangs! I was not meant for this!

I repeated in my mind, fangs, fangs, fangs, hoping that it wouldn't help. To my surprise, it actually did. Why did it have to work?! I felt my teeth get sharper, and the girl noticed to!

As quick as I could, I put my mouth on her neck, and sunk my teeth into her skin. As it happened, she started to scream in agony, and finally fainted. I took my mouth off her neck, and half smiled. That actually kind of tasted good.

Maybe being a vampire wasn't that bad after all, but I still had to see the rest of it. What do you for the rest of the night? Be bored out of your mind?

I jumped up onto the windowsill, feeling a little regret and remorse for what I had just done. It tasted pretty good, but it doesn't change the fact that I just literally sucked the life out of someone!

I looked down at Riley, who now was smiling broadly. Not one of those fake transmittable smiles from Faith, but an actual smile.

I didn't care anymore whether anyone's smiles were fake or not. If they were fake, they didn't like something about me. If it was real, that means that they liked how I did something. Usually when it was a real smile, it was when I was doing something bad.

"Good job!" She smiled with her fangs. "Now, let's hit the clubs!" She pointed away from the large house to who knows where.

"Clubs," I wondered. "Where the heck are those, deep in Clutch woods, or in an old abandoned jail?" I asked Riley suspiciously. By then she was already walking away, motioning me to follow her, which I did. Maybe after I did this she would give me some space, along with the rest of the council. Personal bubble here people!

She flew up, as did I. I loved the feeling of the cold air for this time around oddly. I noticed that the street lights weren't on, but I could still see almost perfectly. That must be another one of my newfound powers. I didn't enjoy the sucking blood part or the stay up all night part. I had to admit though, the powers were pretty cool. Just saying, to me it is pretty darn cool to run 50 miles per hour, let alone like 200 miles per hour after I reach my maximum ability!

Anyways, it was very odd because I was a "newbie," yet I could fly faster than Riley! Even though I could fly faster than her though, I still stayed behind her so she could show me the way. There weren't really any twists and turns, but that was because there was no air traffic for vampires!

I mean that'd be dumb right? Because I really don't know what is what anymore.

We finally landed at the back of a rundown restaurant. It was small, like a diner, with broken windows. I could see inside that there were flipped chairs, an old rusted counter, and some of the tables were cracked, providing nice homes for whatever wanted to live in there.

Riley led me to the back, where there was a trap door. She opened it to reveal an old rusted stairway. There was a big bright red light coming from the end of the slanted stairway.

I looked around once more, just to reassure myself because this "club" looked very claustrophobic, and noticed there was the border of Clutch Woods about ten yards away from us!

Hey... I know this place! It's Candela's! It was a bar and grill my parents have taken me to before when I was younger!

Before I knew it, Riley had disappeared through the stairs. I decided it wouldn't hurt to try this, besides stopping my overall breathing, but nothing much! So, trying to play the fearless type, I followed Riley down the unwelcoming stairs.

The stairs were very long, and the further you walked, the louder the music became! I finally reached the bottom, and that instant, my jaw dropped as wide as it possibly could. It was a gigantic room filled with strobe lights, restaurant booths, lounge areas, and vampires just hanging out. I'm not talking about five vampires. I'm talking about 20!

How was I scared of this place?

I totally forgot that Riley existed, and instead I was faced with a worse matter as soon as I took everything in.

"Hello, Kylie," Amara greeted me. She looked like a totally normal teenager. She had a dark red top, which was tucked into her black ripped shorts – which were even shorter than Riley's- and black flats. "Forget this place; we are going to Faith's."

"Amara?" I sighed. "What is your deal? Just leave me alone! I did everything you told me to!" I bit my lip. Then I remembered I still had my fangs out when I ripped my lip, and it started to trickle a red river. I took my hand and wiped the blood away so nobody noticed how dumb I was to do that.

Good thing is that thirty seconds later it instantly healed. Once again, at least there was some pros to being a vampire.

"Listen, I don't want any trouble," she said, acting a lot nicer than last time. "I just have to bring you to Faith for no more than ten minutes, and then I'll leave you alone, okay?"

I groaned. "Fine."

Amara zoomed up the stairs like it was nothing, and being myself, I just walked, not rushing myself at all.

Once I arrived at the top I stared Amara in the face with a dead face. "Let's just get this done with!" I pushed off as hard as I could and slowed down again so that Amara could show me the way this time.

In seconds time, we both landed in front of a shack, the one I was dragged to before. Amara grabbed my wrist and opened the shack, and there was another stairway. She pulled me down it.

I gasped, it was amazing. It was a large entryway, filled with maids and servants rushing around. Right in the center, was Faith.

Why did all cool vampire things start with an old rusty stairwell?

This world is so much different from the human world, even though it is hidden inside the human world.

"I've been waiting for you guys," she said like a normal person, "especially you Kylie." Faith added with a creepily inviting voice.

I gave her a funny look, "Why me so much?"

Why was everything "me" so much?

"You're new, I need to take a test." She motioned me to follow her, which I did worriedly. She led me down long corridors, with Amara by my side.

"A test of what?" I couldn't help wondering.

"DNA," they both answered at the same time.

"You see, there is one girl out there that has special DNA, which makes her have double the normal abilities." Amara told me.

"Okay," I said while we entered a room that had lots of machinery. It kind of scared me because it was really pointy and sharp. Faith led me to a chair, and told me to sit down. Instead of the cheap ones I sat on when I was here before, it was a nice arm chair, which surprisingly looked comfortable.

I sat in it, because I obviously had no choice, like usual. It was more like I was a servant than a guest, sometimes.

Faith brought over a small machine that was on a cart, which moved freely because it had wheels on the bottom. The machine however, had a sharp point sticking out, and below that was a metal imprint of a square, just waiting for the match to be paced there. On the other side was a small screen, I noticed.

"It won't hurt that bad," Faith answered the question she knew was stuck in my head. She grabbed my hand, pulling out my pointer finger. With her other hand, she grabbed a plastic square piece that matched up to the imprinted one on the bottom. She held the square under the point, and with her other hand she slid my finger across the point, making blood ooze out of my finger. The stream of blood all fell into the plastic square, which Faith matched up another square just like it, and snapped it shut. She placed it in the metal imprint, and then walked over to the other side to look at the screen.

Faith frowned, and Amara ran over to her as fast as she could. Amara closed her eyes and sighed deeply. When she opened her eyes again, they were her normal blue eyes, and they were turning a shade lighter. Her eyes were filling up with tears.

Why was she crying? There really wasn't a valid reason she should. Who knows, maybe the vampire who tried to come out as tough, was sensitive!

"It was negative," Faith told me. "That means you aren't the one with the doubled amount of powers."

Deep inside, that kind of disappointed me. I mean, I knew I would have to be a vampire forever, but it would be nice if I was stronger than all the others!

"Go now," Amara pointed to the door, with tears streaming down her pale white cheeks at a fast rate.

I did so, but on the way out, I swear I heard the words "I thought it was her," coming from the mouth of Amara.

As I slowly walked away, I heard someone scream.

"Wait!" Faith ran after me, and gave me cold stare. "I forgot to discuss the punishment." Faith brought me into the nearest room there was, which happened to be a bedroom it looked like. It was very very large, and it looked even bigger because there was no bed.

I frowned, "why do I need another punishment? Wasn't it punishment enough for biting me?" I crossed my pale arms, thinking about all the terrible things she could do to me. With an odd new confidence that had just popped up, I stared her in the eyes. I wasn't afraid of her anymore.

"No, that was not a punishment!" Faith groaned, after that her facial expression changed, as if she were having an argument with herself about whether to punish me or not. "First of all, you need a punishment for your little act of rebellion! Seeing since you love the little vampire scene so much, I've decided that I'll give you a little lesson for a while." She smirked one of her famous smiles while being sarcastic. It looked really weird.

Oh my gosh, will she stop that permanently?

I sighed, "I guess I don't have a choice."

"You're darn right you don't," she said. "Come back here in an hour, and we will start right away!"

"Can't we start now and get it done with?" I wondered aloud.

"I suppose if you really want to." Faith moved over to a chair. "Sit," she commanded as if I were a dog.

Knowing that this person could make my life miserable, I followed her command, and sat, like the dog everyone thought I was.

"Hmm..." she tapped her chin.

I smiled broadly. After this, then they'll leave me alone.

"I'm only doing it so that you know the basics, so it's not exactly a punishment I suppose." She told me.

"Okay, Faith, now could we get on with the point?" I asked with a touch of eagerness, so I could merely have it be done.

"Sure," she gave me another hard stare. "First of all, you call me Ma'am."

"I thought you were the vampire leader... Ma'am, and I kind of figured you wouldn't be so uptight." I stated.

Okay that is crossing the line here! I would say something if I had the power to, but nope! I was still the newbie.

She eyed me suspiciously as if I were some kind of monster. "Well, Amara is second in command. I am first in command." She paused to make sure I was following. Once she realized I did, she resumed. "Third in command is Mason. And fourth in command is Cassidy. For Cassidy it is Ma'am, and for Mason it is Sir obviously. Amara doesn't like to be called something formally."

I nodded along, getting slightly interested. So, at least all I need to remember is to call three people Ma'am and Sir! How hard could that be, though still I didn't want to do it?

"That includes following every order they give you, but as I've seen and heard you are very good at that," Faith chuckled a bit.

Hmm, maybe that is because I was forced to?

"I thought you weren't traditional?" After I asked that, an even better question sprang up in my thoughts. "Have you been watching me?"

"Calling people by their rank is normal, even in the normal side of the world," She answered. "Kind of like in the army, plus, why wouldn't you show respect to someone who could do pretty much anything they could imagine to you, no questions asked?"

"And no, I have not been watching you, but when you've come to see me-" She went on.

"Against my will," I interrupted quietly, but this was a vampire, it probably wasn't quiet to her, especially when her powers reached the fullest.

"Thank you for demonstrating being disrespectful!" Faith said sarcastically.

"Sorry Faith," I apologized. "Ma'am," I corrected as soon as I recognized my mistake.

"Something tells me this may take a while," Faith said, willing to go on, which she did. "If you do not treat these people the right respect, your reputation will go downhill fast. Trust me; it takes a while to get a really good reputation."

"Why do vampires want good reputations?" I asked her, hoping to get a darn good reason.

"It's been noticed they enjoy their lives more." Faith looked me in the eye, "Kylie, right?"

"Yes," I nodded. "It is kind of funny how you knew my name before, but your just asking that right now, isn't that right Ma'am?" I threw in the Ma'am this time on purpose to demonstrate my point.

She rolled her eyes a bit, "Maybe so, but I don't like putting in time to remember lowly newbie's names'." She rudely stated. "So, moving on, vampires don't sleep, they can eat human food also, but it won't taste as good as it used to. Vampires also can go out in sunlight all they want. Oh, and I bet you already know what garlic does."

Oh, I surely do!

I guess it's good that this lesson happened, because she just cleared up almost all the vampire myths for me.

"Also, I thought you should know each vampire has their own strengths and speeds. So you could be stronger and a little faster than others vampires when you reach your maximum or maybe you won't. It depends on your level of athleticism when you were a human," Faith explained.

Maybe that's why I could fly faster than Riley. She wasn't all that athletic as a human.

Faith commanded me to get up, which I obviously followed now knowing the risk of not doing so. "One last thing, only I live here, but you'll find Amara, Mason, and Cassidy here a lot." She walked out of the door, motioning for me to follow.

This time, we walked all the way to the other side of this palace like place, to see two doors on either side of the dead end corridor. Faith knocked on the right one first with her skinny knuckles, opened the door swiftly, and gave me a slight push in.

The room was rather small, with nothing in it but a chair, which was strangely the most popular item in this place.

There was also a girl about my age walking over to the door. She had golden blonde hair, many freckles, and a kind face. Her clothes were a mismatch of a red and purple top and bottom.

"Hello Cassidy," Faith greeted.

"Hi, Ma'am," Cassidy replied back, not even thinking about it, just having the word Ma'am roll off the tip of her tongue. She than looked at me, her smile faltering a bit, I saw her try to cover it up with a fake cough, which made it even more noticeable. "Who's this?"

"This is... Kyla...Kylie! This is Kylie!" Faith exclaimed. That's weird, considering she didn't want to remember my name!

I held out my hand, "Nice to meet you... Ma'am."

"What's that?" She acted like she didn't hear me, prompting me to say it louder and clearer.

"Ma'am," I answered her request. I could tell already I didn't like her, seeing that I could already tell she was a power freak.

Hah, what am I kidding, they were all power freaks!

"Well," Faith started while she backed up, out of the room. "I better go introduce her to Mason." She gave me room to back up as well, just when there was a person coming down the corridor.

The boy looked sixteen, having scruffy blonde hair, glimmering blue eyes, and wearing a casual T-shirt with jeans. He stopped right in front of me, looking me up and down.

"Mason this is Kylie." Faith introduced us.

I had to admit, he was pretty cute. "Hi, Sir," I said, almost saying Ma'am.

"Is this the girl you were talking about?" He asked Faith.

"Yep," Faith answered and started to walk away, and as she was doing it she yelled. "Session's over, you can leave now."

I turned around, and started to run away, hoping to get out of this place as fast as I possibly could.

"Hey, you!" Mason shouted.

I stopped instantly, come on, when could I leave? I turned around, "I thought Faith told me session is over?"

He ignored the question, "Come back here?"

"Yes, Sir," I said in a small voice, than ran back over to him in a blur, and he moved to the side just in time so that when I was stopping, I would hit the wall instead of him. I got up hazily, and looked into his eyes.

"You're a newbie, eh?"

I nodded fast, wondering why he had just asked me that question. Wasn't it obvious?

"The one who survived a vampire attack, and then decided to be a vampire hunter," He put quotes around vampire hunter.

Come on! That was a bluff... kind of.

"Faith only punished you by helping you know the basics?" He asked himself. "That does not sound like Faith, one bit." He continued to speak to himself, than he looked at me, with his eyes bearing into me. "You- whatever your name is- you're going to help me."

I cringed.

"You are going to help me figure out why you are so great in the eyes of Faith."

Chapter 6

" W HAT IN THE world do you mean?" I wondered aloud.
I don't really think I'm on Faith's good side, but if so, I really don't want to see her bad side.

"I mean, Faith usually never gives anyone a punishment like learning. Just asking, what type of punishment is learning?"

I bit my lip, "School. Well, maybe they are just coming around, you know?"

He sighed, "Never mind, you can go," he waved me off.

I was going to say something, but then I decided that it was probably not wise of me to ask why he would care, so I just ran off, undisturbed.

I ran out of the place as fast as I could, feeling relief once I had escaped. Sadly though, I hit another person as I tried to weasel my way through the woods.

I fell over, but the person who ran into me was still standing straight up, scornfully looking down at me. "Kylie! Where did you go?" The voice seemed mocking, and sincere at the same time, and I just plain did not understand that.

After I adjusted to the darkness again, I realized that it was Riley! For one time in a while, I was actually happy to see her, kind of. "Amara kidnapped me." I groaned. It's kind of funny though, because I made it sound casual, like every day it happened.

She gave me a weird look, "Well… okay!" She gave me her cold hand, to help me get up. I took it, not gratefully though. I was still mad at Riley, and Riley decided to make no attempt to make amends, no matter what. It seemed like she used too, but now she didn't care at all.

"Thanks, I still have a lot of issues with running." I chuckled a bit. Not one of those, oh, were best friends again, nothing ever happened, chuckles. It was the type that I was trying to be polite to a random person I didn't know. "It doesn't help it keeps getting faster."

"About that… Did you pass the DNA test?" Riley wondered. I could tell that her tone was wavering, as she tried to make the topic seem casual.

"No, what about you," I asked in return, even though I really didn't care, at all. I was actually trying to find a place where I could just say "bye", and then fly off. But, Riley started to run her mouth again, before I could say I needed to leave. I decided that I would say "need" instead of "want", because it would sound better.

"If they are still doing the test that means the vampire hasn't been found." She tilted her head to the side. "Didn't they tell you that? There can only be one female vampire who has that extra power in their DNA." She gave me a look that made me feel arrogant, so I decided to give it back.

"Oh, whatever," I shrugged it off. "Anyway, did they tell you that vampires can't drink Coke because it has some ingredients of garlic?" I lied, hoping that it wasn't obvious that I was bluffing, and making it seem like I knew something she didn't!

I chose to say Coke had garlic in it, just because that used to be her favorite drink, and I doubt she would just give it up like that, even though she was a vampire now. I mean, I'm a vampire, and I haven't lost my insanity or personality!

Riley looked surprised, "Really?" At first she looked doubtfully at me, but as she saw I kept a straight face, she decided I was telling the truth.

I guess it was a good thing that Riley wasn't that bright, or else she totally would have known I was lying.

"Faith gave me the basics of vampires." I bragged, trying to make it sound like it was actually cool, when it really wasn't. "Plus,

I ran into those jerks Mason and Cassidy." I rolled my eyes, then looked at Riley, trying to make sure she was listening.

"Cassidy equals jerk, but Mason? Huh, he must not like you." Riley smiled, probably because she finally found something to sting me with.

"Yay," I said sarcastically. "Amara doesn't like me, Faith doesn't, Mason and Cassidy too." After I said that, I beat myself up about it. It gave Riley another chance to zing me again, even though the first zinger wasn't so great.

"Well, after all, they all have reasons not to, like I do myself," She smirked. "I really don't blame them for it, honestly. First of all, it's your looks. Second of all, you have a terrible personality, and who likes that?" It was her turn to laugh now, which she complied to do.

"Okay, Riley, I get it," I said through gritted teeth, cutting her off as well. I did my best not to show her I was actually kind of offended. Although I don't know why I was offended in the first place, considering that Riley only said that stuff out of pure anger.

Riley started to walk towards the shack, and as she did, she did not try to be discreet, kicking fallen leaves and branches on the ground on her way. "I can go prove to you that Mason is nice to me, he just plain doesn't like you." She stated, probably silently noting that I didn't believe her when she had said it a minute ago.

"Oh, it's on," I squinted my eyes of hopes that it made me more intimidating, but that's when I realized that Riley had her back towards me, and she was already walking down the shack stairs.

Then, following suit, I jogged to the shack, and walked down the stairs as well. I went down the stairs in the same way as last time. In awe.

When we reached the end of the straight stairs, there was Mason, waiting there for an odd reason. He looked like he was waiting for someone, and I had a feeling it was Riley, seeing how his expression changed when he saw her.

"Hello Riley," he greeted kindly to her. Than he looked at me, "Hello as well," Mason said again, kind of rudely.

I smiled a fake one, "Thanks that makes me feel really good!" I exclaimed sarcastically. I could have easily added his name-sir- but I decided from now on I would try to stay away from calling them by their "names."

They may be "important," but they aren't royalty, even Amara.

Riley stood there laughing silently, seeing that she had just proved she was right. That made me kind of mad, seeing I never did anything bad to the guy, and here, he doesn't like me!

Riley now laughed a bit louder, trying to make the tension between the third in command and I a lot more obvious, even though it was already pretty clear.

"Oh, by the way, I talked to Faith," He said, trying to lead me on. I stood there waiting for him to go on, in which he didn't. He just pretended to get lost in his thoughts purposely, just to tick me off, and frankly, it was working.

"And?" I rolled my fingers as to say, "Get on with it already!"

"All she said was that you needed a lot of extra help." Now he didn't even try to sound like he cared!

I bit my lip, "That's nice to know!" I lied, feeling the need to call him something, and trust me; I had lots of options I was already scrolling through in my mind, starting with jerk.

I walked on forward, hoping to get away from this rude, strange guy, who had good looks. I don't know where I was planning to go, seeing this house was very large and I already forgot where everything was. But as long as Mason didn't know that, I think I would be fine.

"Oh, yes, keep walking straight, then take a left, than another left, than go down the stairs, because that's your room." Mason instructed sarcastically, meaning that it was probably full of psycho killers, 'cause that was the type of person Mason seemed to be.

"What is it, a death trap?" I challenged. I walked up to him and got about five inches away from his face. "Now leave me alone!"

"What's going to make me?" He challenged back, possibly hoping to get the better out of me, but if I'm going down he's going with me!

"What in the world are you two doing?!" A familiar voice yelled at us. I turned to look at Amara, who was getting mad. Okay, that was a little under exaggerating. She looked like a red balloon about to pop and scatter into tiny pieces.

"This jerk here won't leave me alone!" I backed away. I looked at Riley for help, but she just turned away, and started to laugh again, but louder - a lot- louder than last time. That gave me another forgotten reason I was mad at her.

Amara yanked on my shirt, and pulled me with great force away from Mason, "You better watch it," she growled at me, and after that her fangs popped out, plus her eyes turned red.

I turned towards him, "Yup Mason, Amara is being super nice to me right now!" I stated sarcastically. I shouted that mainly to show Mason that he had no idea what he was talking about, and he really should leave me alone, for good.

Once I get my full powers, they are all going to regret ever pushing me around.

I felt like once Amara found out I didn't have the special DNA she didn't like me at all, showing me no mercy. Maybe she was being extra hard on me because "she thought I was the one?" I mean, what difference would it make though?

"What'd you just call me?" Mason asked me.

"I'm sorry!" I whimpered. Of course I just walked into the dead end I wanted to avoid with the whole formal names thing.

For some reason I always ran into those ends.

Mason pointed his pointer finger towards the ground, as telling me to go to the floor. I did so, following orders as I usually did with my new life. I didn't enjoy it, I just did it. I don't want to do it, but I know it's better if I did, so I don't get into worse trouble.

I stayed sitting on my knees while Amara looked at me thoughtfully. Finally, she grabbed my head to look at her, which I was doing already. "From now on, I would recommend to not act with your personality, because nobody really likes it." She looked at Mason without letting my head go.

I really don't care! Of course I couldn't say it… Wow. They really did have lots of power over vampires. I guess I know why they were picked for the job.

Riley walked up to Amara and patted her on the back. "You know, I totally agree." Both girls turned my way, grimly smiling at me.

I had to ask myself why I was even her friend in the first place. She was always a nutcase, ever since elementary school.

"By the way," Mason started, "I know you aren't like the others. I don't know why, but my gut instinct is not to trust you, so therefore, nobody will." Mason looked at me with mean eyes that tore up my insides.

So the only reason Mason doesn't like me is because of a stupid gut feeling?! Wow, that's not a very smart outlook to life!

When I was younger I had a gut feeling that Ari was going to be a nice child. Now was that very accurate? I don't think so.

Amara smirked at his comment, "Mason's instincts have never failed before, so they aren't going to fail now. So if I were you, I would spill it before we spill you." Amara threatened.

Riley whispered something so quiet to Amara, which I couldn't hear it, but I had a feeling Mason was supposed to hear it as well, somehow. After that brief moment, Riley ran away, leaving a blur in her spot that quickly disappeared, along with Riley herself.

That was yet another time when I felt unbearably helpless, especially when I was supposed to know something, but I didn't.

"I don't know..." I honestly said. "I don't know what I ever did to upset Mas- Sir," I quickly covered up. Dang it! This whole name thing was not working for me! "Please," I begged. "I would tell you if I knew."

I saw Amara and Mason exchange a glance, deciding what to do with me. When they finally turned back to me, Mason smirked. "Then you need to prove it."

I gave the two a puzzled look, "How?"

"Oh, we are just going to ask you a couple questions," Mason answered. "How long have you been a vampire?"

"A day," I gulped. How was this supposed to help? I didn't know, but it still freaked me out.

They both exchanged another glance at each other. I hope they were telling each other that a day doesn't give me much time to go do something really bad.

"What have you been doing for that past day?" Amara asked me loudly.

"Not much, just being stuck with Riley and the vampire council." I looked down, waiting impatiently to leave.

"I suppose there may be another way," Mason said, "Because we'll never squeeze anything out of her this way." He crossed his arms strictly.

"Thank you!" I actually allowed myself to smile. I stood up now.

"Not that we trust you still," Mason stated. "We'll get it out of you eventually, just not now." He paused for a second, allowing me time to catch my uneasy breath. "That's why you should worry when your powers are maxed."

I turned to walk away desperately, but Mason stopped me, again.

"Hey, where are you going?" Mason asked while he grabbed my arm with his vampire strength. "We aren't done with you yet."

I groaned, "Fine, but can you just please let me go soon?" I pulled away from "sir" until he finally let my arm go.

"I guess the only thing to do now is to bring her to Faith," Amara told Mason, while she was looking at me disgracefully.

"Isn't she doing something important?" Mason asked almost in a whisper, obviously not wanting me to know what he was talking about.

Amara crossed her arms, "Well I think that this matter is more important, Mason! Who knows, she could be working undercover for the Red."

They both looked at me, and I just shrugged. "I honestly don't know what's wrong with me!" I admitted, once again. I kind of rolled my eyes in annoyance. "I would have told you by now!" I popped out my fangs, which also turned my eyes red. "Besides that, I need to get home soon."

They escorted me deeper inside the building, which was the opposite thing I wanted at that very moment. Finally after walking for five minutes, we saw Faith in a room which was rather small, that only had a large marble table in the middle. There were black chairs surrounding it, so I took a seat.

"I thought I told you that you could leave," Faith groaned.

"You did, but these lovely others thought otherwise," I told Faith sarcastically. I leaned back in the black leather chair, trying to get comfortable, knowing that this was going to take a while. All of the full vampires around me noticed how I leaned back in the chair, but nobody had the heart to say anything about it, oddly.

"Why?" She asked like the matter was very unimportant, but it was actually to these two numbskulls behind me.

"There is something different about her, it's a gut feeling. I don't believe we should trust her. We already tried to get it out of her, but she claims that she has no idea what it is. And like I said, she should not be trusted." Mason explained briefly.

"Um, excuse me, but, um, I really have no clue what it is, and I have a feeling that this is turning in a very bad direction," I stated broadly, hoping that my voice would be heard, even though I was a newbie.

Kidding! I doubt they care if I'm a newbie or not.

"See?" Amara contributed to the conversation. "She acts as if she has no idea what it is-"

"Because I don't," I interrupted. They all stared at me with their eyebrows raised. "Sorry," I said under my breath. "Go on."

"I mean, she could be working for The Red for all we know." Amara finished, leaving me hanging. Who in the world is The Red? The only answer that popped into my mind was vampire hunters, who actually know of their existence, in which, I could care less, honestly. I didn't even want to be involved with the vampire world, but frankly, it's too late for that now! I was the focus of these three jerks! I decided, once I knew how to use my powers, I would get back at them somehow.

'Cause all the odds right now pointed to proof that they were bad, not a trace of good. If they wanted to get on my good side, they would leave me alone!

"I don't think she is working for them, because have they ever actually done that before? You know what their goal is, and it is stupid, unnessicary, and impossible!" She told Amara with her gaze pointed at me. "Plus," she added even quieter, "I've been taking a liking to this girl."

All of our eyes, especially mine, widened as much as they could at this shocking, but good news. Well, the news was good for me anyway.

"That is why you're free to go now, and I'm going to have a little chat with you two," Faith smirked. Mason and Amara were even paler than before, with their mouths wide open.

I laughed in happiness, "You two better close your mouths, you don't want to attract flies." They both gave me death stares, which said "watch your back."

I ran out of the odd room, out of the shack, than took off for the comfort of my own home. I've had enough vampires for the night.

Chapter 7

I LANDED ON MY driveway in one swift move, trying not to land too terribly hard on the pavement, for that would make too loud of a noise. If that would have been the case, I more than bet that one light in the house would have flickered on, enveloping me in doom. If my parents ever found out that I had so much of opened the front door at night, I would have ended up grounded for a month. Now sneaking out of the house at night for about three hours, that would result in probably being grounded until I was eighteen!

I started to walk up to my front door, than I stopped myself. What was I doing? I couldn't risk going through the front door again! It creaks too loudly, plus if my parents have discovered I was missing, they could catch me right at the door. But... if I went through the window, I could get in with ease —seeing I left it unlocked- and, if my parents knew of my absence, I could always psych them out by saying I was in my bed the whole time.

I ran over to my window, realizing that was a big mistake. Actually, big wasn't a good enough word for it. GIGANTIC, was a better word for it!

I was getting faster, and at a fast pace as well. I estimated I was at about seventy miles per hour right now. That was bad, because at seventy miles per hour, hitting the side of your house makes a pretty loud smacking noise.

I lay on the ground, just wanting to stay there forever. The pain was so bad, but healed so quickly. I was amazed by it and grateful as well. By that time I felt well enough to get up, and sure enough to take my time. But, all those great feelings quickly died away as I heard the front door open with my stunning hearing, and I saw a dim light heading my way.

I had thirty seconds to a minute to figure out how to get into my window without harming it. The time was ticking down fast, as was I as I climbed the side of my house to my window on the third story. When I looked over to the dim light of a flashlight as it got larger, I only had a matter of seconds. I could tell it was my Dad by his heavy footsteps, and his wavering breath.

I finally ripped off the screen, pushed open the see through glass, and hopped inside just as my dad approached. I heard the screen hit the ground, and the sound of my dad jumping because of the unexpected surprise. Just before I closed my window, I heard the low mumbling of my dad.

"Huh, must have just been the wind shear."

I closed the window quietly, than chuckled under my breath. When would he realize there was no wind?

I walked this time around, all the way over to the short distance of my bed. Even though vampires don't sleep, I still thought I should lay in the comfort of my bed. Plus, if my parents come into my room, wouldn't it seem suspicious to be seen standing around?

Anyways, the last couple hours of darkness gave me time to think about what had happened tonight. I mean, it was actually fun! I was also less conscious than I thought I would be, and I guess that's a good thing. I mean, I shouldn't stand around feeling guilty for what I am. I guess it's good that it was fun, seeing I would have to do the same thing over and over for the rest of my life. Well everything was pretty fun except Mason and Amara.

I know they were pulling my leg before, but they weren't kidding about not trusting me, and I knew that pretty certainly. And, something told me, that that was going to cause me many issues, seeing they were second and third in command of the vampire world.

On the other hand though, Faith liked me- or was she toying around with me too? I know I have never done anything to her that would make her like me in any way, starting with disobeying her when Riley kidnapped me the first time.

Riley. Even just the name got me angry. Why would she expect me to make amends with her so quickly?! She doesn't tell me she's a vampire, she lied and lied and lied, she kidnapped me, and she badmouthed me a ton! How is that supposed to make me forgive her? For all I cared now, was that Riley was an enemy, and that was it.

As my thoughts made the time go by fast, the next thing I knew it was 5:00 in the morning. The sun was coming up slowly, and if you looked really closely, you could see blurs every once in a while, from vampires who were edging it close. I could probably only see it now though, because of my great eyesight, but in the eyes of a mortal, they would see no more than dawn.

I looked thoughtfully at the world around me. I could live this way. I mean, look at me. I was enjoying it, and I fit in already, having already made my allies and enemies as well.

Since my parents usually don't awake for another three hours, at least, I guess I could possibly go stretch. I hopped out of bed willingly, and walked over to my dresser carefully. Before I was to run again in an important event, I needed to practice. Every time I ran, I shouldn't always go and run into obstacles, like a house, a wall, a person, a door, a tree, etc.

I opened the dresser carelessly, which was an obvious mistake. I forgot I had super strength, so the whole dresser almost fell on top of me. It wobbled a ton, and I had to calm it by holding onto it for a matter of seconds. This time around, I opened it like a feather, and pulled out some running shoes, black leggings, and a red baggy Bears sweatshirt from past school events.

I threw it all on, plus an added red headband and I put my long black wavy hair into a ponytail.

After that, I opened the window, put my foot on the window sill uneasily, and then glanced around making sure no one was watching me. A matter of seconds later, I felt content that there was no human eyes' following me... But... I was scared to hop off the window sill. I pushed myself out, flying with the wind, wondering why I was so worried! I was great at flying! It was the best thing for me with my new abilities.

I knew I had flying down, but strength and running was really hard to maintain. I had no idea how Riley got it down so fast!

I landed at Verona Park. I realized there wouldn't be any people at a park at 6:00 AM, so I thought that it would be a good place maybe just to control my running at least.

I also needed to tell myself I couldn't be scared to run. I mean, I jumped out of a three story window! I'm pretty sure running is nothing compared to that!

I positioned my body on the far side of the big park, so I had a while to run, which obviously wouldn't take long to do. I was just about to start to run, but then I hesitated. I spent three hours in my room, which meant I was even faster now. I started to doubt myself, telling myself that I still needed to do it. How about I just start slow? That should work...

I sprinted quickly, but not as fast as I could, probably around twenty miles per hour. While I needed to stop, I knew I would jolt forward like I usually did, so this time I estimated how far I would jolt forward, so that I would end where I wanted to. It worked! I stopped where I wanted to, but at the end I couldn't really keep my balance, so I fell over onto the lush green grass.

I sat there for a brief minute, thinking about how I could keep my balance at the end. I kept thinking, yet I couldn't figure out what could cause me to stop. So, eventually I decided it just took practice. If that didn't work, I would just need to run into an object every time. I would be okay with that, because it didn't hurt me for long, but what if another vampire saw me doing that? It would be embarrassing!

I pushed myself up, and ran to the other side again, pushing myself to run at fifty miles per hour. I knew that wasn't very smart, but I really wanted to jump ahead. I estimated once again, and it was odd because I actually stopped running ¾ the way there, and the force of it pushed me to the designated spot, but still, I fell down. My brain kept shooting me down because I couldn't control my balance, but I always tried to make myself feel better by saying I was pretty good at the estimating part. Not that I was being cocky or anything.

I started to wonder if I was even doing it right. I had one more idea on how to run, but after that I was out.

I ran hopefully over to the other side, once again, but instead of estimating, I stopped myself at the designated spot, and used my super strength to resist the urge to go flying forward. Once I did that, I immediately smiled. I didn't fall down! I was perfectly straight, standing up! I silently congratulated myself, until I smelt something.

It didn't smell as if it were Riley, it smelled like my food last night! That must mean that there was a human nearby. That quickly ended my little practice, along with my good mood.

What if this human saw me using my powers? I honestly didn't want whatever it was to go through what I did. So that left me no choice, but to walk on, like I didn't notice anything, as if I wasn't a vampire. I was a perfectly normal girl. Yup.

I thought to myself quick before walking off. I should be able to fly home after I couldn't smell him. So I started to walk in the direction of my house, even though it was like, four miles out.

I walked past a pine tree, and then I heard a CRUNCH, from a snapping twig or something of the sort.

"Hello?" I asked, started to get a bit shaky, seeing if there was a person there. Then a bad thought came to mind. Hopefully, that twig was loud enough for a human to hear. It may have been loud to me, but I obviously had really good hearing.

I kept walking, at a fast pace, wanting to get out of there desperately. After a couple minutes, I got on an uneven trail.

I must have walked a half a mile already, but yet the smell didn't go away. That means the human was following me...

I finally turned around angrily, and shouted. "Stop following me!"

Behind a nearby tree, a boy popped out, slightly embarrassed. He had dark brown hair that was a bit overgrown, messy at that. Plus, he had dark green eyes that stared at me hardly. He had slightly high cheekbones, with full faded red lips, and a crooked nose. It wasn't that crooked though, you could hardly notice it. His skin was tan, and he was skinny. His arms were muscular, not too much, but more than Mason. And, he looked to be about a year or two older than me.

Regardless of his barely noticeable crooked nose, he was cute!

I looked at him coldly, "Spill it." I tried to put the tough tone in my voice, like Amara did when she pretty much threatened to kill me.

"Uh..." He started, "I'm just, ah, um... looking for my dog." He looked around uneasily, "Um here, um, doggy doggy?"

"Are you sure?" I raised an eyebrow, "It's name is doggy?"

He shifted uncomfortably, "uh, yes, yes. DOGGY! Come back doggy..." He acted as if he were actually looking for his "doggy," pretty poorly at that.

I falsely looked at my nails, acting like this was no biggie, but in the inside I was screaming on what to do next. "Seriously, not buying it," I fixed my gaze on him again.

"Well..." the boy locked his eyes with mine. "I was wondering where you were going," he said anxiously.

"Why?" I asked instantly after he finished his last word. "Why did you want to know where a random girl was going?"

The boy looked down, his cheeks turning bright red, like a tomato. "I noticed you were pretty..."

"Oh, well that's great," I said, showing him I didn't necessarily care. "I hope you know that stalking a girl isn't going to make her like you."

He bowed his head a little, as to say, "I get that."

The mysterious boy was still a distance away, and I wanted it to stay that way. If that guy was to advance a step further, I was seriously thinking about biting him.

I waved my hand in a dismissive gesture, "now shoo!" I know I was being unfriendly and rude, but I couldn't just let anyone into my life now seeing I was a make believe creature!

"Okay..." He turned around to walk away. "Oh, by the way I'm Chase. You are?" Chase asked, being friendly, even though I was being a jerk to him.

"A person who you shouldn't be talking to," I answered. I hoped it didn't make me sound cocky and I thought I was better than everyone, but I was doing this for his sake. If we were to become friends, his life would take an unexpected twist.

He turned around and gave me a shy smile. "Bye" and he ran off the opposite direction.

Just his words and his look made me feel there was something off about Chase. He seemed friendly and open, but mysterious at the same time.

I slowly felt his smell go away, and that gave me the cue I could leave now. I walked to a nearby oak tree, and pushed off the ground. At incredible speed, a minute later I landed in front of my front door, and I walked in happily. Home seemed to be the place to be at the moment, especially after the creepy run in with Chase.

I wondered what I was going to do during the day, seeing night was my time. I guess just hope my family is doing something entertaining! I smiled at my own mistake for a moment. When could my family ever be entertaining?

I was walking to the kitchen at the moment, and then I stopped.

Wow. It had only been a night, and I was like a completely different person now! Now I actually thought vampires were okay, first of all. Well, besides Riley, Mason, Cassidy, and Amara... Those four vampires weren't the highlight of my life. They were like four disasters waiting to happen. Except I can't say that, because it had already happened!

I looked at the kitchen timer on the oven, and it read 6:34. I just sat on the chair for a while, thinking about the events of the morning...

I hadn't done much for the entire day, and it made me feel antisocial, and I'm sure my parents thought the same.

I decided that for the rest of the summer, I should probably find a friend, or at least someone to hang out with. That already narrowed out all the people in my life! The only other person I could think of was Chase... I realized if I just made it seem like I was totally normal, than maybe we could hang out, regardless that I'm a vampire.

It was 11:00 PM, and everyone was soundly asleep, so that I could sneak out with ease. I repeated the steps before when hopping out the window, except this time I made it seem normal. I flew all the way to a Lakeshore house, because I liked getting revenge on these rich brats. It brought me pleasure.

Not just because I was a vampire.

I repeated these steps as well, and this time when I broke into the house, I felt I could easily run, but not full speed. Just about fifty miles per hour seemed good. I ran all the way over to the door in the large room, and locked it, seeing it was already shut.

I popped my fangs out, and hissed, awaking the boy about seventeen.

He rubbed his eyes, and tried to see the image of me disappear, as if I were just a fragment of his imagination. "Why is there a child in my room?" The boy asked me with a touch of rudeness to his deep voice. Kidding! It was more than a touch. It was a seeping handful.

I ran over to him and bit him almost immediately, obviously not wanting to start a chat about why a soon to be eighth grade girl was in his room.

After I was satisfied, I jumped out the window again, and flew to the park again. Once I landed, I was surprised to see vampires messing around all over the place. At night, it was like a completely different world for the big town of Verona Park.

I was astonished all the sudden though, to see all the vampires hanging around, to just fly away in a blur. It looked so cool. It was this huge burst of air, just rushing up towards the top of the night sky. And as a vampire I could see all the different blurs departing their own ways.

Why did they all leave at the same moment though? Did word already get out that the council didn't like me or something?

That's when I realized it wasn't me. It was good and bad news.

A dark figure came out of some pine trees. I tried to find his features, but I couldn't. The figure was in a black cloak, which covered up most of his face, so no vampire could recognize him. If it was even a him. The figure held a small gun, which was loaded with... garlic?

It seemed pretty stupid, but if that garlic was to touch any vampire, it would paralyze them, leaving the black figure to come get them.

As I smelt the fragrance of the person, I could instantly tell in was a human. A successful human vampire hunter as it looked.

As I got lost in my thoughts, the figure was looking at me, targeting me to be exact. As soon as I realized that, I instantly stared at him.

I don't know why I didn't notice him targeting me, since I was the only vampire there! Why was I so oblivious sometimes?

"What?" I asked innocently, pretending to be human so maybe I could somehow avoid being his next catch. Unlike the council, he didn't believe my lies.

The figure didn't buy it, I could tell easily. It was as obvious as the fact that black and white are different colors. Or maybe even more obvious.

He aimed the gun at me, and in amazing speed, a clove of garlic came hurtling towards me. Out of pure fear, I ran away as fast as I possibly could.

I could run at about one hundred miles per hour now, but I didn't want that. Not knowing how fast I was going, I missed the giant oak tree in my view, so I whacked into it.

I fell to the ground, and was about to get up, but the vampire hunter was fast. Too fast. The garlic was already hitting my face, and I was already breathing in a terrible stench.

Chapter 8

I AWOKE IN A small confined room that had a hard floor, which I was laying on. It was dark, but I could still see perfectly. I notice there was an old light hanging from the ceiling, and as soon as I noticed it, it turned on.

I could hear footsteps coming my way, but I couldn't move my head, or any part of my body. That's when I saw the garlic clove on my stomach, resting easily.

The black cloaked guy hovered his face over me, realizing I was awake. I couldn't see his face though, because he had a ski mask on as well.

"Hello sunshine," the figure said happily, probably because he caught me. His voice was deep, like many voices I've heard before.

"Hi," I mumbled, remembering that I could move my lips. The light above me was starting to get very bright, which annoyed me a lot. I wanted to complain, but then it struck me that it wouldn't make a difference. "Let me guess, first catch ever?"

"Nope," he laughed. "You're my sixth." I could sense the seriousness that had crept into his voice, which also made me realize that this person could be no more than 15 years old.

I finally got right to the point, "What do you want with me?"

"Nothing much..." He trailed off.

"Seriously, couldn't you be content with the other five?" I wondered, hoping that he didn't notice that it was supposed to be a little rude.

"The other five didn't last," the mysterious figure said. I think he sensed my eyes pop out of my end, "I didn't kill them," he told me reassuringly. "But I could have," he said warningly.

Frankly, that didn't make me feel better, knowing that he could have killed me already, and that he still could kill me right now.

"Just tell me what you want," I groaned, hoping that I could get out of this place as fast as I possibly could. It was bad enough having to deal with the council, but him now?

"First of all I want your name," the boy said. Although I couldn't really make out anything on his face, I knew that he wanted the truth from the way I could feel him looking at me.

I turned my eyes away from him in shock. I knew who he was. I scratched my brain as much as I could for my name. Finally I turned my eyes toward him.

"My name is, 'a person you shouldn't be talking to,'" I answered simply, and Chase started to chuckle bitterly as he turned around and started to pace.

"You're a smart one, you should know that." After he said that though, his voice turned dead cold, "Except maybe you should tell me your real name."

Realizing that my fate was in his hands, I told him, "Kylie." I looked down at the garlic on my stomach, "Can you take this off of me now?"

Knowing that it took time for the affect to wear off, he took it off me, but held it threateningly at me. He took off his ski mask, and let his eyes stare me down for real now.

"Thank you," I tried my best to smile, but it was fairly hard seeing that I was still paralyzed.

He laughed at me, as he saw what I tried to do. "So now you open up?" He wondered while he gave me a look that told me I had to tell him.

I sighed. "Look, I'm a newbie. I've been a vampire for two days now, but I've known about them for about four or five. Those couple days I knew about them, and wasn't one of them, I was constantly worrying, knowing they were going to come after me." I explained as he nodded along. "I knew if I had let you into my life, you would probably figure it out. I didn't want you to have the same thing happen to you." I stared at him, hoping that it would be a good enough reason because it was kind of a lie. It wasn't the total truth, but hey he didn't have to know that.

"I guess that's a valid reason." He said while he stopped pacing. "I knew you were a vampire when you were practicing your running," he laughed again. "You were pretty entertaining."

I twisted my face up in wonder, "Then why didn't you tell me that?"

"I knew you would have bit me," he admitted. "I saw the gleam in your eyes that you weren't afraid to." He folded his hands, trapping the garlic in the middle. He sat down in a nearby chair that had more garlic on it. He pushed it all off and sat down.

As I slowly recovered, I sat up, looking Chase straight in the eyes.

"So I guess that means you didn't think I was pretty?" I asked, making it sound a little more serious than I thought it would.

"Gosh no," he looked at my face and smiled a little. "That part I wasn't lying," his cheeks turning a light color of red. "Anyway, going back to the whole point," He steered away from the other subject. "I captured you, because I thought you would be of use to me." He held up a hand, telling me not to ask. "Feel up to par at getting back at one of your rulers?"

I smirked, "Always."

Chase actually seemed quite surprised with my response. "I thought you liked them, seeing you're one of them." Chase stated. "Don't you like, suck up to them and do all their bidding? Call them Ma'am, Sir, and in return they treat you like crap?"

"Yes, and just because I'm one of them doesn't mean I like them. Faith is okay, I suppose, but I wouldn't believe in those stupid stereotypes," I said, recalling when Faith said she liked me and me especially hating Mason and Amara when they forced me to listen to their issues. They're all like, "you need to treat me with respect or else I'll hurt you," I said in a mocking voice.

Chase laughed again, "You said it better than I." He smiled at me, knowing this would be fun for me now although he probably would have smiled anyways if I didn't want to.

"Go into Faith's shack, and find Amara. Tell her you think that you think you know the vampire who has the special DNA, and bring her back here." Chase ordered. "By the way, I'll show you where to find this place in a minute." He added quickly. "By then, I should have a decoy placed in here. Once she is in, close the door, and lock it. It is super strong, so vampires can't break through it." He stood up, motioning me to stand up too. "We'll leave her in there until sunrise, where than she'll have to rush to cover." He smirked, "sound good?"

I laughed back, "great." It was perfect, it wouldn't harm her, just severely annoy her, and I was fine with that! Maybe a little more than fine, AWESOME!

Chase dropped the garlic on the floor, feeling he could trust me now. "Now, let me show you where this place is..."

I followed him willingly, liking the idea of making Amara angry. He showed me where it was quickly, and then looked at his watch.

"We'll do it another day, it's already 4:00 AM."

My eyebrows rose, "I was unconscious for five hours?"

Chases nodded, and led me back into the small room. He told me to sit down, and he started to talk again. "I hope you know that everything isn't all great between us."

Well, I kind of knew that anyway seeing he KIDNAPPED ME! It was kind of a shame though, because if I hadn't known that Chase was a vampire hunter- a good one at that- we could have been friends now since I knew he isn't this stalker giddy boy. He was still a stalker, just not a giddy boy.

I nodded along, listening to every word he said. "Just a question, why didn't you like tie me up or something? You just left me on the floor, where I am free to move?" I wasn't complaining, I just asked it out of pure curiosity. It was just a little weird.

"Well I had garlic, and I could still kill you," Chase pointed out again, emphasizing "I could kill you." That just showed me he knew what he was doing, and he really didn't care whether I was friendly or not.

In this situation he kind of went back and forth. One minute he was being kind of nice, the other he was warning he could still kill me!

I took a deep breath, "Okay then..." I pushed myself up against the brick wall, so I could let my back rest. I noticed that Chase saw me moving, so he was ready to strike, and for a moment, I thought he would. What happened to that trust I saw a moment ago?

Wow, it kind of seemed like he was nervous since his attitude was changing so much. Was he lying about me being his sixth catch?

"Don't worry," I put my hands up. "Just going over to the wall," I rolled my eyes.

"Better be," he said under his breath. "Just because you're happy with helping me make Amara mad, that doesn't mean I like you."

"I noticed," I told him in an impatient voice. "Now when can I leave?"

"In a minute," he told me softly. This told me, no matter how many times he told me that he could kill me, he never would.

Wow, this guy was really confusing!

I decided to ask a question that had been bugging me for a while. "Chase, why are you a vampire hunter?"

He looked at me, with a half questionable face, the other half surprised. "I want to scare them into hiding, so they will stop hurting people." He looked at me with an eye raised, almost to ask me if I did that.

"I mean, it's just the way they live," I stood up for the kind for an odd reason. "We can't help it," I gave him a sad smile. I shifted uncomfortably as I saw Chase staring intently at me.

"I guess I could give you a chance," he gave me a half smile.

That made me smile a happy smile for a moment, but then it quickly vanished in a blink. Chase was talking about me, not the race. Huh, what did you know, we both had a soft side. That quickly faded as he strictly added a few words under his breath.

"Only, if you are good."

Yes, yes, yes. I get that. I'm a dog who belongs to Chase, Faith, Amara, Mason, and Cassie. I'm seriously like a family pet. "Oh Kylie, you better behave or else you're going to go to the kennel!" Or, in Chase's way, my head detached from my body!

I nodded solemnly, "Yup yup yup! I know that already." I rolled my eyes again.

Chase raised his eyebrows, "excuse me?"

"You've got to be kidding me, another jerk." I said so quietly, that Chase could barely hear me. "Sorry, Sir..." I trailed off, knowing that this is another Mason, but a touch nicer.

Chase stared to laugh. "I'm kidding! Do you really think I want a pet vampire?" He bit his lip, knowing that I thought he had really meant it, and I was more than annoyed. "No Sir," he added quickly, knowing that he forgot to say that.

I happily stood up. "Now, that's the way I like it." I gave him a short smile. I knew this was a long shot, but I was desperate. Very desperate. "Want to hang out tomorrow?" I rambled quickly.

It was official. I belonged in a mental facility. Asking him, "Do you want to hang out tomorrow?" actually means I was asking a vampire hunter if he wanted to be my friend! Did I just forget I was a vampire? I hope so, because that was a stupid question for a vampire to ask.

Chase looked at me with a face that was clouded with questions, but only one popped out. "Depends, can I bring my friend Simon?"

"Well," I started. "Does he know that you're a vampire hunter and I'm a vampire?"

"No clue," Chase smirked. "As far as he is concerned, he thinks I just found a pretty girl. He's clueless." He walked closer to me in a fast stride. "You willing to play the part?" He joked.

Did he like me? He just called me pretty!

I blushed and stood up in a quick movement to seem like I didn't notice he called me pretty. "Sure," my pale face brightened widely in amusement. "So today at noon?"

"Great," he told me. "I have some hours to catch up on sleep since I caught you." He rubbed his eyes for a second.

"Well to make it obvious," I laughed bitterly. I walked over to the door and looked back at Chase one more time. "See you later," I gave a fast wave. I ran out of the brick shack slowly, so I wouldn't hit a tree like the last time.

After I had run a good distance, I looked back at the shack that was only a speck now, and thought of Chase. For someone who kidnapped me, he seemed nice. A little bit too nice...

Chapter 9

I T HAD TO be about 4:30 AM, and I was freaking out. Last night, I nearly got caught! I landed a block away from my house, so I could just take my time, without any rush.

I looked around at all the nearby houses, wondering if any of the people were vampires. It could be possible, seeing there was a ton of vampires that lived in Verona Park.

My thoughts were quickly disrupted, when I sensed a human coming. Very abruptly at that.

I flew up quickly, so the person couldn't know what I was, or more importantly, who I was. I landed at the side of my house, scrambled into my room, and plopped on my bed like the night before.

Man, I needed to work on my stealth skills! If even a human can sense me coming, I'm really bad at this. One thought still always hit me hard though. What if the human did see me? Nah... I doubt it, I told myself over and over.

Before I knew it, it was noon, and I was at the park. When I was flying, I spotted Chase behind a tree, looking for something. I blurred down by him at ease, and noticed that he didn't flinch.

"What's wrong?" I asked making it seem like flying was casual for me now.

Chase looked around cautiously. "They are on to me," he said really quietly. After looking around for another minute or so, he turned towards me. "The council, I mean, they don't know it's me specifically, but they know that there is a good vampire hunter out there." He walked out from behind the pine tree. "I guess I need to lay low for now. I can take one vampire, but the whole society doesn't work my way."

I scoffed. "You're telling me." I walked with him, and then I realized something. "Why do you smell like nothing?"

I could always smell humans, vampires, and whatever there was I've learned from the past days. Chase didn't have a smell though.

He pulled something out of his shorts pocket- a tiny bottle. "Special vampire hunting item makes you smell as if you're not there, so you can get closer without being noticed." Chase explained briefly, as a big smile corrupted on my face.

"Forget about Amara! Tonight, we are breaking into Faith's shack," I smirked as I just got that idea.

After a moment, Chase caught on, and my smile spread to his face. "12:00 tonight, we'll meet here again, and then, discuss our plans."

"What plans?" An unexpected voice piped in.

I looked the way that the voice came from, and standing there was a tall, thin boy, who had brown glasses, blonde hair, a dark blue T-shirt, and light blue shorts that went to his knees.

"Oh the plans..." I looked at Chase for help. He just shrugged, leaving me blank. "The plans for... um... today!" I stuttered unsurely. I turned my head back to Chase. "We'll talk about this tonight." I mouthed, referring to our earlier conversation.

Simon looked surprised. "Chase, you mean she's with us?" He shifted towards me awkwardly.

Chase gave him a meaningful stare that obviously said something. I couldn't understand it though, since I wasn't up to the latest teenage boy code.

I backed up from Simon a bit, since he was totally freaking me out. "Yeah, the first thing on our... plan was to... swing on the swings!" I held up my thumbs and smiled weirdly.

Okay, I was not going to get used to this soon.

"Actually, Kylie, I thought we discussed going to the grocery store," he eyed me, trying to tell me something. Something like... garlic! He was unarmed, while the council was targeting him! He needs garlic!

"Yes, sorry I forgot!" I mumbled, catching on. We all started to walk towards the grocery store in silence. The grocery store was about a mile away, so we figured we would be okay.

I was in the middle of the two walking down the path, because Simon decided that I had to be and Chase couldn't, so I was stuck walking by Simon, who was staring at me. Seriously, that isn't making him seem desperate at all!

Simon yawned obviously, getting closer to me and put his thin tan arm around my shoulders.

I ripped his arm off my shoulders and stopped walking. "You ever do that again, and you're dead," I warned him. I didn't mean it, but I almost did.

We started to walk again, and I swear, like five more times Simon tried different ways to get closer to me. He was creepy! Creepier then Chase when he kidnapped me for sure!

Speaking of Chase, I looked over to him who was trying to not notice the awkwardness between Simon and I. Chase actually seemed pretty cool even though he was a vampire hunter and I didn't know him that well. Plus, he was kind of hot.

After a while, we entered the grocery store, and went straight to the aisle with garlic. Chase grabbed a bag and stuffed tons of garlic into it, so I figured that he was out of garlic at home, or he was very paranoid.

I was going with paranoid, since that's what I did when the council as after me!

While me, being my vampire-y self, stood a distance away since I wasn't used to so much garlic this close to me. Ever since I had been a vampire, the most garlic that had touched me or was around me was a clove. This was about fifteen whole garlic bunches, with like, fifty cloves!

Chase noticed me standing back at the other side of the grocery store, and also saw that Simon was looking at me odder than he was before! Simon walked up to me and laughed.

"Why so far away from the garlic? It's not like you're a vampire!"

I laughed nervously. "No, I just really hate garlic, it smells bad." I said half truthfully, even though there was a lot more to it than that considering his joke was right.

"You know, you could just wait at the next aisle, not the other side of the store." Simon pointed out, and tried to shift towards me again.

If I was waiting in the next aisle, I would be barfing! I could still smell the garlic over here! But of course Simon didn't know that...

"I should go..." I turned around and walked out of the door. Gosh, he was creepy, weird, human... ugh. Chase wasn't creepy, a bit weird and human... I still liked him a ton more than Simon.

I waited outside for the two boys to come out, and finally they did. Chase had a bag of garlic, and so did Simon. They both had their bags slung over their shoulders'. Chase did a good job staying a distance away from me, but Simon here, wasn't too bright. He was sticking to me like glue!

Chase's gaze was set forward, in a hard lock. I could tell he was embarrassed for his friend's behavior, and frankly, I was too!

After we had walked a good distance, I couldn't take it! I swear the bag touched me twice, and the scent was killing me! "You know what Simon?! It's called personal space!" I moved over a meter, hoping that would help a little, but it didn't. And do you want to know why? Simon moved over with me!

I rolled my eyes, and gasped. When he moved, the plastic wrap that was the bag ripped, leaving all the garlic flowing out of it. And one landed on my foot.

I was forced to be still by the garlic. But my eyes weren't, so I glanced at Chase, because this time he needed to save my butt!

Simon was standing beside me, with a puzzled look on his dorky face. "What are you doing?"

"It's a game Kylie and I play. Random moments we freeze... yeah it's not a very good game." Chase said on the spot.

Is that really the best he could come up with?!

I groaned softly, knowing that I was in a pretty bad predicament. I looked at Simon, who was looking at me with a frown.

"If it's not a good game then how about you keep on walking?" Simon asked with a rude tone. He glanced at Chase, who was now silently freaking out.

"You know, I think it's time for you to go home Simon," Chase dismissed. Chase pushed him towards the nearby neighborhood. Simon walked away, grumbling to himself and looking backwards towards us angrily. It's not like we cared though!

I sighed in relief. "Thanks," I laughed. "I never thought a vampire hunter would be helping a vampire!"

Chase bit his lip. "Well, I usually don't even hang out with them!" He looked me in the eye. "Now since he's gone, maybe you won't have a shadow." He walked over to me, bent down, and started to pick up the garlic that had never been picked up.

After a couple minutes, the affect wore off, and we went about as if nothing had ever happened. We started to talk about our plan, got into great details actually.

"No no no no no," I argued. "You are not going in her shack. They'll kill you in a snap of their fingers." I stared into Chase's green eyes. "I'll go in, grab it, and run out. I've gotten better at running as long as I'm not freaking out," I recalled when Chase was hunting me, and I hit a tree in fear.

"Kylie, keep in mind you're a newbie, you can run faster now." Chase pointed out. "If you hit anything, it will sound as if a drum was being hit, except it would hurt."

I raised an eyebrow, "How are you a vampire expert?"

Chased sighed loudly, "My dad is a vampire. He killed my mom, with his fangs."

My smile faded as I heard his depressing story. "How did you find out it was him?"

"I witnessed it." He admitted. "I was nine, I didn't know what to do, so I called 911, told them my mother was shot." He pondered for a moment if he should carry on. Knowing that he could trust me for real, he went on. "My dad tried to stop me, but it was too late. He fled, leaving me for social services." He looked down, his eyes turning transparent from his single tear that ran down his cheek. "After that, that's when I realized that he had no choice. According to records, he died seven years ago."

My throat was dry, so I couldn't say anything. So all I did was grab his hand and squeeze it to reassure him. "I'm sorry," I squeaked.

No wonder the kid could get out so much. He had foster parents!

"It's okay," he told me. "Anyways," he said, trying to change the topic. "If you're going to run, you need to practice."

I nodded in reply, and stood up from where we were sitting under an oak tree. I put my black wavy hair behind an ear, and ran to the other side of the park. I could run about two hundred miles per hour now, like any other vampire. I caught on pretty quickly, but had to practice a couple of times.

"I'm good," I said with no hint of being exhausted. "Meet you at your little death house at 1:00a.m., with our targeted item?" I joked around, bringing a smile to Chase's face.

"You know it." He handed me the tiny bottle. "Keep it; you'll need it if you are on my side."

"Thanks," I told him gratefully. "This will come in handy when I'm stealing the DNA tester."

It was dark out. It was my cue to leave. I climbed out my window once again, and flew into Clutch Woods, and started to wander around until I finally found the shack.

Okay, I can do this. If they can catch me, it won't matter, right? They already hate me- well, except Faith. She's bound to sometime, considering I have a gut feeling Mason's theories don't go away quickly.

In a ridiculously fast motion, I had opened the door ran down the stairs, racing towards the room that held the DNA tester. The door to the DNA tester door was open, so I rushed in grabbed it, and ran out. The DNA tester felt insanely light, for some odd reason. That's when I realized I'm a vampire! It should feel that way.

I sprinted out of there, to the outside woods. As soon as I reached the forest, I pushed off the ground and started to fly towards Chase's little hideout.

Once I was there, I let myself in to see Chase waiting patiently. "So how'd it go?!"

I smiled, not feeling exhausted one bit. "Maybe the DNA tester will tell you!" I joked. "I think it went rather well considering I have it and I did it in less than a minute."

"Set it down there," He pointed to a tiny foldable table that was barely as big as the DNA tester. I set it down, looking proud.

"I did it!" I exclaimed happily.

Chase smiled, "yes you did."

I bit my lip as my stomach rumbled. "I forgot to eat though." I popped out my fangs. "I'll be back later," I gave him a smirk.

As the next week passed, I got to know Chase a whole lot better. Plus, my vampire powers reached the max, so I was no longer a newbie! I was kind of surprised though, seeing I felt like I could run and fly faster than a normal vampire, so finally one day when I was hanging out with Chase, I asked him something I probably would never think twice about.

"Do you know how to work the DNA tester?" I asked, hoping the answer was yes. "I want to be tested again," I looked down and started to mess with my pale vampire fingers.

"Yes, but why do you want to be tested again?" Chase wondered as he pulled me into the small building.

I bit my lip "Well, don't call me crazy, but I think I may have the special DNA, even though I already tested negative. It could make sense because what if you have to have your powers at the max?" I suggested thoughtfully, while Chase pricked my finger on the machine.

"That is a good reason," he agreed. He let the flowing blood fall onto the square just before it instantly healed. He snapped the matching square on top of it, and placed it on the metal imprint like Faith did for me before. Chase ran over to the other side of the machine, and bent down to read the results more clearly.

He gasped, and that made me freak out. "What?! What did it say!? I asked in suspense.

"It was… positive." He breathed. "That means, I just figured out who the strongest vampire in the world is." He looked into my eyes and smiled. "I should be terrified right now."

I rolled my eyes at his joke. "Just 'cause that proved positive doesn't mean I'm any different than before. My personality is still the same!" I walked over to the other side and looked at the other side just to make sure he wasn't pulling a prank on me.

He was right though. The small screen had a large plus sign on it proving it positive, and he really should be terrified!

"I can't wait to tell Amara and Mason! Ha, it will be hilarious!" I laughed. I looked at Chase, and found my laugh and my smile disappearing.

"You shouldn't tell them unless you need too." He told me. "Right now, it's just between you and me because if they find out they'll take you away."

"Why...?" I wondered, knowing where this conversation was heading.

"They will want it for themselves," he said firmly. I saw his mouth twitch, as if possibly he were lying. I dismissed that thought quickly as soon as I realized I trust him more than anybody. I may have only known Chase for a week, but he knew my secret, and I knew his. And the fact that he hasn't tried to kill me yet proved a lot about him.

Plus, he wasn't that bad looking either. I already knew I might have had a tiny crush on him, but just a little one! Maybe.

I grabbed Chase's hand, and dragged him out of there. "Well it's just between us then," I smiled with my fangs out.

"Where are we going?" Chase asked in a nervous tone.

"Outside," I told him simply. "It's getting dark out, so I should probably get home, and so should you." I gave him one last look, and pushed off the ground with such great force I went flying in the air, at incredible speed. I thought sometimes at night it was fun to fly slowly, just to take in your surroundings.

All was peaceful, until I saw something that was so unbelievable, it even scared me! I stopped in midair, spectating the scene below me. It was a cop, who pulled up to a kid- it had to be a vampire-sucking blood of a human on the sidewalk. But what it had to look like to a cop is a kid beating up another one.

I landed behind a nearby tree, and watched what happened.

"Hey, kid! What do you think you're doing?!" The cop asked as he got out of his car.

The vampire just froze after he took his fangs out of the other kid and quickly put them back, along with his red eyes.

"Uh…" The vampire shrugged. "I just found this guy lying on the ground after someone beat him up?" He tried miserably.

I noticed the vampire had to be about sixteen, and he had blonde hair, blue eyes… it just dawned on me who it was. It was Mason!

"I'm sure I believe that," the cop said gruffly. "I saw what you did there… you bit him." He walked closer to the body that lay still on the ground unconscious.

"I didn't bite him," Mason lied unconvincingly. "I beat him up," he told the cop instead.

So first, another kid beat him up, but now Mason did? If I was the cop, I would have already arrested him!

Well I suppose it's better to get arrested for beating a kid up, instead of revealing the whole vampire race, Sadly though, the cop didn't believe him. I didn't blame him for not.

"No you didn't, there isn't any bruises. You bit him- in the neck." The cop bent down to examine the victim further, and he noticed the two holes in his neck. "Kid, get in the car!" He barked at Mason.

Mason couldn't fly away now, seeing that would expose the entire vampire race. Frankly, now, he was going to be brought in and interrogated for what he did, and eventually, they would find out that vampires were real, and even though I was only a vampire for about a week now, I couldn't let that happen.

I ran as fast as I could over to the cop ordering Mason to get in the car, and grabbed his head. I pulled his head down to my knee, when my knee was rushing towards it with great speed and force. It made good contact, making the cop go unconscious. Not dead and have mental problems for the rest of his life, but just unconscious.

The cop fell to the ground, moaning softly. Now since I saved the entire vampire society from exposure, I decided it was time to gloat.

I turned to Mason. "You're welcome," I smiled.

"I could have done that myself!" He argued, crossing his arms angrily. "I don't need a little thirteen year old girl stalking me and fixing all my issues.

My jaw dropped. "First of all, it didn't look like you were going to do anything to the cop. Second of all I wasn't stalking you. I was flying back to my house, and noticed an inexperienced vampire get in trouble with the law!" I clenched my fist, ready to strike Mason in the face. I decided not to, considering he already hates me, and I hate him. "Bye now," I gave him a fake smile. I pushed off the ground, and flew fast back to my home, desperately wanting to get away from Mason.

About a minute later, I landed behind the tree in my front yard, and walked up to my front door angrily, and let myself in.

"Kylie, where have you been?" Dad asked as I walked through the door.

"Hanging out with Chase, why?" I wondered as Dad looked down at me disapprovingly.

"Riley came over earlier, looking for you." He told me. "She said that she needed to talk to you immediately, but I couldn't tell her where you were, seeing I had no clue." He crossed his arms and he gave me a stern look. "Leaving notes on the counter at 9:00 AM saying you went out isn't working for your mother and me anymore." He pointed to Ari. "Tomorrow, you need to watch Ari from 8:00 AM to 5:00 PM. Mom and I need to go to another work meeting."

I groaned. "Why can't you buy a babysitter?"

Dad chuckled. "Well they cost money, where you don't." After that last comment, he left me in the entryway, even angrier than before!

Then, a smirk crept onto my face. Well then he would be happy if he had two babysitters, right? And that second babysitter would be Chase.

I'm guessing what the urgent news Riley had was the little crime I committed. So I had to be ready to tell Chase. I mean, that would be the only reason, wouldn't it?

I didn't really care if she knew or not, and I doubt she actually knew, considering from past experience. Like at school, we could have a week heads up for a test, and Riley wouldn't realize it until the day before!

I walked up to my room calmly, ready to wait until 11:00, when I would be safe for sure. When I walked into my room, though I gasped, it looked like there was a whole crowd looking for me. There was Riley sitting on my window, dangling her feet out of it right next to Amara who was doing the same. As for Cassidy, Mason, and Faith, they were waiting for me at my doorway.

"Hello," I greeted, wondering why the heck they were all here. This couldn't be the DNA tester thing, it was too important. "Why are you guys here?"

"The DNA tester is gone!" Amara angrily stood up from the windowsill like Riley did, and came crowding over me like the rest.

I raised an eyebrow, "So?"

"It is very meaningful, and whenever I find out who stole it, I'm going to crush them!" Amara screamed at the top of her lungs.

Okay, telling them it was me was way out of the picture now, even though I never planned to have it in the picture. "Quiet down, princess." I said that not in the term of respect, but in the term of your being too picky, demanding and snobby.

All of them seemed to ignore the fact that that was how I responded, seeing they were all beyond flustered. All of the sudden, I got a pang of curiosity in my body, making me ponder a question that I haven't even thought about yet.

"Why is it so important? It is just a machine," I pointed out. Sadly, since this regarded the stupid DNA tester, Amara noticed my edginess in my question, just like Riley would use.

"That's none of your business," Amara growled at me. She popped out her fangs and looked into my eyes which were now red in return. "Maybe I'll tell you when you're not so unimportant," she hissed. She looked away from me, probably giving a mental note to treat me as less then she already did.

I hissed in return, and watched as all of them left my room in a big blur, sending a huge gust my way, making me get a chill up my spine.

After I put my mind back into the real world, I pulled my phone out and started to text Chase. "Come over to 342 Warwick Drive tomorrow at 8:00 AM to help me babysit my sis?" SEND!

A few minutes later, my phone chimed. I pulled it out and read the message. SURE ☺

I laughed at his smiley face. It was not manly.

After that brief moment of relief, I looked out into the night, which was now completely dark, and frowned to myself. I knew that eventually, I was going to get caught. And face Amara's punishment.

Chapter 10

I HAD JUST EATEN, and I thought maybe I'd go check out the council's progress. I desperately hoped that one of them wasn't a secret detective or something, or else I was dead meat for sure. As I peeked into a conference room where the council was sitting, I was grateful for the bottle of whatever it was that Chase gave me so they couldn't smell me.

My eyes quickly widened as I saw they were just a step closer to finding it was me. They knew it was a girl, rebellious, vampire. Most importantly, they had a photo. One of their guests got a picture of me, and they were now trying to un-blur it to figure out it was me.

In total and utter fear, I ran as fast as I could out of there, to the safety of my own home. The safety of my own home though was quickly diminished as my bedroom light was on, and I turned it off when I left. I thought maybe if my parents walked out for a second, I could slip in and pretend I was always there, but they were just looking around my room in distress.

So I needed to walk in through the loud front door. I slipped in with one very slick and stealthy movement, but the door was too loud. My parents came running down, with a look of anger on their faces'.

"Where were you?!" They demanded at the same time.

"I just needed a quick whiff of fresh air," I lied, biting my lip in nervousness. That's when I realized I still had my fangs on. That meant I still had red eyes. Blood dripped in my mouth because I dug my pointy fangs into my lip. I buried my head in my hands for a moment, turning back to my human appearance, even though I still had the same amount of threat. I really hoped my parents hadn't noticed, because if they did, it would have been the end of the line for me.

"Yes," Mom said sarcastically. "That's exactly why you changed out of your pajamas. Go outside and smell the roses, hmm?"

I nodded, "yes, actually. That was what I was doing. Thanks for the concern," I smiled innocently at them. "I wasn't out though, I just needed a quick breath," I hugged them both. "Good night!"

I ran upstairs in a fast movement, realizing after the fact it might have been too fast, but I doubt my parents noticed. They were too busy trying to not believe me about the whiff of air, which they were right.

Relief came over me as I spit the blood out of my mouth and into my garbage can. It was sending an odd, distasteful feeling all over my body. The part of my lip I slit with my fangs had already healed, but that doesn't mean that the blood just vanishes into thin air! Human blood may be good, but vampire blood was gross. Disgusting in fact!

I hopped into my bed and pretended to sleep for the next couple of hours, so I wouldn't risk my identity or get in trouble. Soon enough my parents had left and Chase came over.

"They caught on that fast?!" Chase asked me as I just explained what had happened the previous night. "I'm sorry I made you do that," he apologized.

I smiled. "That's okay; I wanted to tick them off. It's so fun!" I laughed. I hopped off the counter and watched the living room, seeing that's where the little devil Ari was. "Anyways, thanks for helping me with Ari, she can be really tough to control sometimes."

Like on command, that's when Ari started to scream. "I want my dolls! GO GET ME MY DOLLS!" Ari demanded loudly.

I dragged Chase in the living room, and got startled, which is sort of hard when you're a bloodsucking beast.

"Now, Ari if you behave, I will tell you a secret," Chase told her.

I raised an eyebrow expectantly at him. "Now what will that be?"

"You'll have to see," he replied.

It was amazing; he was like a miracle worker! For the rest of time Ari behaved like the little angel she was supposed to be! At the end, the secret was even better.

Chase only whispered it to Ari, as he already knew I could hear it from a mile away. "Unicorns are real," he smiled.

Ari's face lit up and she jumped up and down excitedly, her short blonde hair flopping behind her. She gave me a smug smile, as she thought she knew something that I didn't. First of all, I knew. Second of all, it wasn't even real!

"Good job, Mr. Babysitter, how 'bout you go ride your unicorn back to your house?" I laughed at his little "secret" he told Ari.

"Maybe I will," he smirked at me. He walked over to the living room to talk to Ari quickly, and she was still beaming from the big secret he told her.

Right after that, Chase left, knowing how much he'd helped me with her. For that, I was super grateful. He helped me survive for eight hours.

Fifteen minutes later, my parents came home, and were very surprised on how I didn't complain about Ari, and I was kind of too. They never found out that Chase was here since I wasn't going to tell, and Ari had promised if she ever wanted him to come back, seeing she practically worshiped him now.

Since Mom had said if I did a good job she would take me to the mall to get me some new clothes, I casually walked up into my room to grab a sweatshirt. I already had my shoes on, so I would be ready to go!

But I stopped when I walked in though, seeing there was an item waiting for me in the center of my room. It wasn't any object though. It was the DNA tester.

I ran over to it and read a note that sat on it.

We've figured you out. Welcome to your punishment.

I tried to say something, anything, but the only thing that came out was this. "Mom, we can't go shopping! Something just came up."

Then, I smelt something behind me, but there were too many. Five vampires jumped on me, one that included Amara, and I assumed the rest were guards. They forced my hands behind my back, and as much as I tried to resist, it didn't work. Especially since one guard had extra thick gloves on, with a garlic clove held in it. The stench was terrible!

He ran up to me and pulled out my foot, but I was kicking now. The vampires behind me had put something on my wrists, in which I couldn't break out of. All four of them grabbed my feet and made them be still, allowing the one guard to put the clove of garlic in my tennis shoe, so it would stay there, rendering me useless for a long time. For once, I regretted wearing those shoes. If only I would have worn flip flops!

They picked me up, and started to fly, bringing me to Faith's shack in a couple of minutes. Even though I couldn't move, I could still feel pain. That's when I realized that when being paralyzed by garlic allowed you to feel pain, and it did not feel good. Whatever they tied me with was digging into my skin, and when I was in the air, I hit trees multiple times, and they didn't even care. In fact, Amara seemed happy that I was in pain. Why the heck does she care that much about a stupid machine anyways?!

I mean, it seems a little odd. It's just some junky metal.

So by the time I was on my knees in front of the council, I was bruised and battered terribly. I looked up at them, showing no mercy whatsoever, even though I felt like crying and breaking down in front of them.

"So this is your little thief?" Cassidy sneered as she secretly scolded me with her body posture. She looked over to Amara doubtfully.

So I guess it wasn't really a secret.

"I guess I was wrong to like her..." Faith trailed off, showing me no emotion at all as she paced around me looking down at me disapprovingly.

"Plus, I know why I didn't trust her." Mason stared me in my one good eye, seeing the other one was badly hurt, so it was shut. "She was planning to take the DNA tester the whole time."

"I only planned for the day I actually took it." I pointed out. "I'm not that slow." A smirk crept on my face even though I should have been scared for my life. "Besides, I did save you and the entire vampire society when I knocked out that cop."

Everybody overlooked that important fact, as if I were lying. Instead, they hopped right into my punishment! Faith put in her input first.

"Remember when I said I was going to capture you as a maid? Well, I was thinking that maybe a year's work of being one from 1:00 AM to 5:00 AM every night will be enough?" Faith suggested.

Ugh! I don't even like doing chores for my parents! Let only working for these idiots for no pay? No way in my right mind!

"That could work," Amara agreed. "But there would have to be more. Maybe spending a week's worth time in our jail?"

I wanted to rip out my hair! Jail? Sure, let's just throw the thirteen year old girl into a vampire jail cell Amara! I really hated her now.

"We could always have Riley tell her parents they went to their cabin for a week," Mason stated. "That way, she could spend all day there."

I do really not like where this is going...

"It's settled then! She spends a week in jail, and then is our maid for a year!" Cassidy exclaimed. "Now, if you excuse me, I'm going to go have something to eat." She walked out of the room casually, like this sort of thing happens every day.

Mason pulled the garlic out of my shoe, and started to escort me to vampire jail. I noticed that we went straight, took two lefts, and went down a staircase to arrive at the cells. That was where he told me to go when he and I were having our first official fight.

Something told me that random vampires weren't allowed to go down there, so if they did, they might be stuck.

By the time we entered the lit up cells that were old, rusted, damp, and cold, relief came over me as all my injuries disappeared. Mason shoved me into a cell, took off the thing that was hurting my wrists badly, which seemed to be a metal strap thingy. He locked me in, and stood there for a second, having a question hung over his head.

I rattled the metal bars, which were also vampire proof. I sighed and stopped.

"If it wasn't the DNA tester that was weird about you when I sensed something bad about you, then what was it?" Mason wondered aloud.

I knew the answer loud and clear.

"C'mon," he pushed. "You're trapped in a vampire proof cell, you are going to be forced to be a maid for the next year, what do you have to lose?"

Everything.

I remember when Chase told me "only tell them if you absolutely need to." I wondered if I should tell Mason, since I'm pretty sure Chase doesn't want me to be in jail for a week, and have me be a maid for a year. I quickly pushed away that thought. I don't absolutely need to yet. It could wait.

"There is nothing else odd about me," I lied. "You must have been sensing a newbie." I said, hoping it would tie him over for now.

On great timing, Amara walked in, giving me a nasty look. "Why'd you do it?"

I gave both of them a straight face. "I'm not telling either of you until you guys tell me about why the stupid machine is so important."

"Oh, by the way Kylie, I hope you know that starting in a week, you're going to be my maid," Amara gave me an evil smirk. "Enjoy..." she walked away with Mason, leaving me alone in the small area.

There wasn't anybody else in the cells, so that told me they usually weren't this harsh. That meant this had to be really bad... I needed to tell them soon, because I felt it was only going to get worse. Chase said they would take me away, but that would be for a short time, right? Not over a year!

I couldn't even stand the thought of working for Amara, Faith, Cassidy, and Mason. I mean, why should I? They've all been jerks to me. Plus, did it cross their minds I was only thirteen years old?

I slumped up against a rock hard wall. This was a bad idea. And just to do this to provoke the council's feelings? It wasn't worth it, and I didn't understand how I didn't see it before.

But... that is when I had opened my eyes to realize that my actions can come with punishments like this, so I shouldn't tell them. I had to face this without sweet-talking myself out of it by saying I had took another blood test and I was positive. That doesn't mean I'll be a suck up to the council, I just won't be a thief.

For the rest of the night I scolded myself for what I had done, and I felt now was a good time to talk to Amara. I still didn't like her, but I guess it would be okay to apologize, so maybe my punishment will be reduced.

It was morning, and Amara came in with a small water bottle containing red liquid, which must be blood I inferred once she tossed it to me.

"Thanks," I mumbled. I looked up at her with a face of some remorse. "I'm sorry; I didn't realize that this meant so much to you."

"Well it did," she answered, not telling me why it meant so much to her, in which I would like to know. "And it doesn't change the fact that you still stole it."

"And it doesn't change the fact that it's back in your possession?" I wondered.

Amara chuckled at that fact. "That's right. You know, it takes guts to steal something from the council, and just saying stuff like that."

I opened the water bottle, and took a sip. "Well, what can I say?"

"How good do I look in these shoes," Amara smiled while she put her foot on the bars so I could see them.

"Hmm," I considered it for a moment. Black converses did go well with her overall image. "I give them a ten." I crossed my arms. I gave her a cold smile that reached my eyes. "So, look Amara," I stopped for a second. "Ma'am," I fixed my mistake by myself this time. "If you let me just have a week in here, without needing to be a maid or anything, I promise I'll actually make an effort to impress you, and the council."

Amara smirked at me, "I suppose I could consider it since the subject is learning, and showing a trace of remorse..." She trailed off, and I could feel a "but" coming. "But, you need more, another reason why I should." Amara looked at me impatiently.

I had a reason, a darn good one in fact! I had your special DNA you wanted... but still Chase's words echoed in my head not to tell unless I really had to. I kind of had to though if I wanted a lesser punishment then this.

Ugh! This such a hard decision!

Suddenly, I just started talking, and I couldn't control myself with it. "Actually Amara, I have a reason." She looked at me in surprise. "I have the special DNA!" I blurted out, making Amara's jaw drop.

So much for a secret...

"What?! No, you couldn't, we already tested you..."

"I have the theory that your powers have to reach your max before you can test positive," I stated, still wondering why I hadn't shut up already.

Amara was now pacing around in front of me, processing this information. "No, no, and no! You're a lair, I can feel it!" She stared at me with a blank look on her face. "There's no way you're my daughter."

"Daughter?!" I choked. "If I have the DNA, I'm your daughter?!" I looked back at Chase. He was a filthy lair! Just like Riley...

I ran my fingers through my hair. How could I be Amara's daughter? Just the thought of being related to her made me want to vomit.

She just ran away, coming back a minute later with the DNA tester, and the keys. She opened the heavy metal door and pricked my finger, repeating the earlier steps. She walked to the other side and her face turned even paler. "You, you weren't lying!" She stuttered, and she finally pushed the DNA tester away and looked me in the face, but with a soft look instead of her usual hard ones. She took a step forward and reached her hand over to my hair, ready to put it behind my ear like a mom would.

I backed up in response and tried to say something, but I couldn't. My mouth was dry and I was too choked up to annunciate anything. "I have no idea what you're talking about!" I finally managed to say, but it came out in a whisper of anger.

Amara gave me a sad smile. "I guess you deserve to know." She bit her lip and began to tell me everything. "Thirteen years ago, when I was technically twenty-five, I had a baby, and she was stolen the night of her birth. My husband had special DNA, so once my baby was to become a vampire, she would have that too. I hadn't named her yet, so I had no clue on how to track her. So when I met you, I thought you might be the one because you looked like me, and was strong willed. Once you got negative on the test, I was so angry; I started to treat you like garbage." She had a single tear roll down her pasty white face.

It pained me to say this. "So, when are you planning to take me away?"

She looked confused. "You aren't going to be taken away Kylie, but you do have a chance to join the council and become third command, since you are my daughter."

My jaw dropped as I started to tear up as well. "No," I refused. "You aren't my mom, and I don't want to be a part of this stupid, vicious council!" I backed up into a corner. "I'm not sure if you realized this, but you're too late! You had your chance with me, but you've lost it now!" I crossed my arms in disgust. "I may be your biological daughter, but physically, we are different in every single way there is." I stood up. "So as for now, I want nothing to do with you." For a moment I considered just walking out, but a better way came to me. "May I go Ma'am?" I suppose a butt-kissing daughter could get me out of here, now couldn't it?

She pressed her back against the jail cell door to let me walk out. "I'm really sorry for this. Can you please forgive me?" She begged as I stumbled past her.

I turned back to her with a bitter look in my eyes. "It's going to take more than that, but I guess if you want a start, it begins with not telling anyone about me." I turned back away and ran out as fast as I possibly could, dodging all the servants, maids, guests, and corners there were. Wow, it really helped with my training practice!

After I ran outside, I stopped. My parents weren't expecting me for another six days to be home. I looked up into the morning sun and sighed. That means I wasn't going back for six days, because I needed alone time. But first, I need to talk to Chase. He lied right to my face! They weren't going to take me away… they were going to have me as one of their council. That's when the answer struck me hard. He said that because he didn't want me to become one of them.

He still lied though! And I needed to talk to him about it!

I was about to start running, but an unwelcoming figure stopped me abruptly.

"What are you doing?!" Mason glared at me with a stern face. "Aren't you supposed to be in the jail?!" He grabbed my arm with a tight grip, and I didn't have the power to fight back after what had just happened.

"I've been dropped of my charges..." I trailed off, trying not to talk about this, but Mason didn't believe me, so he went further into it.

"Why would Cassidy, Faith or Amara release you? We've never released a maid from these circumstances before." Mason stated, while leading me back into the shack I was doomed to.

"Look," I wiped my damp face with my free hand. I may have managed a few tears without knowing. "Amara decided to let me out of the jail because I was showing remorse," I lied.

"But you still had a maid charge to her." He looked into my eyes. "I'm sure she wouldn't release you of that." His voice sounded cold and hard, but his eyes were soft somehow, almost like he felt bad for me.

I looked down now knowing that he wasn't going to let me go for now, so I just mumbled in a soft voice. "Yes Sir," I followed him now.

When we entered, Amara was standing in front of us, waiting for Mason, not me. When she saw me she downcast her eyes, and her face was even wetter than mine. You could tell that she was taking it worse than me, because at this point it seemed like she was letting herself go, unwilling to fight the power.

"Did you release her of her jail charge?" Mason asked Amara.

"And her maid charges," she told him, not letting her eyes reach his.

Now both of them looked at me. Amara was sad, and Mason was looking at me like, "What the heck did you do to her?!"

I bowed my head. "Thank you Ma'am." I turned to leave once again, but Mason stopped me AGAIN!

Did butt-kissing get me nowhere now?

"Wait! Doesn't the whole council need to agree?!" Realizing that, he grabbed me again and brought me to a conference type room where Cassidy and Faith were chatting. Both instantly stopped when they saw me with Mason and Amara.

Even though my mom was on the council, it was really starting to get on my nerves. Can't any of them be independent and be able to make their own decisions? Because from what I've seen, the council is just one machine glued together.

Everybody sat down after they led me to the other side of the room so I couldn't escape. I probably could if I had the heart to at the moment, but I didn't. I couldn't.

"What did she do this time?!" Cassidy wondered as she gave me a nasty look.

"Nothing! Just leave her alone," Amara fought. "I released her of both charges, but Mason disagrees."

Maybe Amara wasn't taking it worse, because it seems now like she's regaining her old self, fighting against people, except this time, it wasn't me. It was for me.

Faith smirked to herself as she knew this next question would figure everything out. "Why did you release her of both of the charges when you have never done that to ANYONE before?" Faith put emphasis on the word "anyone." Her eyes bore into mine even from across the room. After she'd done this, I felt in a complete world of darkness, and not the good kind. "You gave a vampire from The Red a year in jail, and permanently working here. You never released him, so why her?"

Amara looked back at me, asking approval. We both knew if she didn't tell them, I would have to go back, and have the punishment possibly worse.

I nodded in agreement still hating her, but I knew she cared for me. Then I scoffed. Wow, I had a secret for about ten minutes.

As Amara turned back to the other council members I noticed how much she looked like me. And how young she was, she was nineteen when she was bit.

It was kind of weird to know she was actually thirty eight.

I laughed grimly to myself as the council carried on.

I pushed away the distraction as Amara started to talk to the other council members. There was no turning back now since they saw our little conversation just then, which was just with our facial expressions.

"Guys," she sighed. "Meet my daughter."

Chapter 11

"WHAT?!" MASON ASKED in shock. "She's your daughter?!" He glanced back at me disapprovingly. "Or did she force you to lie, because she is pretty manipulative."

This is where I piped in. "No Sir," I said simply as soon as he said that. I was kind of surprised I remembered "Sir," but that was a good thing I suppose.

"No she didn't. It turns out that you need to have your abilities maxed before the test could be positive." Amara agreed.

I walked up a little further from the corner. "Well since we have this all figured out now, can I leave?" I asked hopefully, desperately wanting to talk to Chase.

"No!" They all screamed in unison.

Cassidy made a look of disgust on her face. "Doesn't that mean that she is forced to be on the council?" She crossed her arms hoping the answer was no, like me.

"Yes," Faith said to my despair. "She'll take fifth command, since I'm pretty sure Mason and Cassidy don't want to be outranked by a maid."

Amara lied to me! She told me I would get third command, above Mason and Cassidy!

Now since my secret was out, I had no reason to suck up to any of them. I grabbed Faith and pulled her out of her chair, then slammed her into the wall as hard as I could. There was a huge SMACK! And I turned around to see all of the council staring at me, with their jaws wide open.

"Oh, it's not that impressive, now close your mouth, you don't want to attract flies now do you?" I asked with that sarcastic voice creeping up. I held my fist threateningly at them, letting Faith go, and she just slid right away from my grasp falling to the floor for recovery. "Who's next?"

All of them backed up from me, leaving me an open passage. "Bye now," I waved. I walked slowly out, trying to prove my authority to them.

Nobody was going to push me around anymore! I was stronger and faster than them, so why should I try to be nice if they always treated me like garbage?

I walked out of the room with my lips pursed. I was no pushover. Once I was strutting down the hall, Mason ran out of the door.

"C'mon, Kylie, wait!" He shouted after me.

I turned around. "What do you want from me? Or have you already got it?"

He super-sped over to me in a huge wave of wind, and the he grabbed my arm so I wouldn't leave, even though I could if I wanted to.

"Seriously, Mason?" I looked down at his hand on my arm. "Oh I'm sorry, did you want me to call you Sir?" I asked sarcastically.

He released my arms. "Listen, I know you think that we're the bad guys, especially me, but we're not." He told me softly.

I opened my eyes wider in mock sense. "Oh, well that makes sense coming from the guy who wants to rip out my insides."

"Okay, I'm sorry, if that's what you want to hear." Mason finally said.

My hard face softened a little. I looked up into his eyes and saw he wanted me to apologize to him too. He was acting like my Dad.

I finally sighed. "I'm sorry I beat up Faith…"

Whoa, that was one thing I never thought I'd say.

Suddenly Amara blurred to my side, and I realized I was getting used to other vampires super-speeding around me. "Mason, urgent news," she babbled quickly. "Red struck again."

Mason ran his fingers through his hair. "What did they want this time?"

"Kylie." Amara said. Both Mason and Amara stared at me.

I was confused. "Who the heck is Red?"

"A large group of vampires into mass biting," Mason bit his lip. "Bottom line, they want to turn the world into 100% vampires."

"You see, every time a vampire bites a human, they have a 25% chance of turning into a vampire, and if they stay human, they don't have any memory of vampires at all." Amara explained. "With you though, since you are the strongest vampire ever, you have a 50% chance of turning humans into vamps because your DNA is stronger, therefore more infectious."

"And if they had you," Mason added. "Their little take over the world plan will work better."

"But I wouldn't do it," I stated while crossing my arms. Are they not paying attention to me? I just beat up a vampire seven years older than me!

"You would if they kidnapped you. They have their ways." Mason started to pace back and forth past Amara and me.

"How do we stop them?" I asked, starting to get worried.

Amara looked down. "A vampire hunter. I don't suppose you know one?"

"No, I don't know one," I lied. "What would happen to the vampire hunter after though?" I quickly asked out of concern.

"We would bite him," Amara said with no emotion.

Okay, wow. Amara seemed like a robot when she said that. Well, vampire robot.

I turned around. I know Chase lied, but I couldn't do that to him. He was a good friend, and I know why he lied to me. He didn't deserve to be punished like this.

"Listen, I have to go," I looked down, and just walked away, forcing myself not to look back.

"What's wrong with her?" I heard Mason ask Amara behind me. I could still feel the tension between Amara and me, even though I know she was my Mom.

I started to super- speed away, and I zig-zagged all through the forest. After I finally got out, I took off to fly to Chase's hideout. I knocked on the heavy metal door, and Chase opened it as quick as possible.

"Kylie!" He grabbed my arm and yanked me in. He locked the doors. "Where have you been?"

"Dealing with being Amara's daughter," I told him blankly. I saw as Chase's smiley face turned into a deep frown.

"I'm sorry; I knew that if I told you that you were Amara's daughter, you would become one of them." Chase apologized.

"It's okay; I still don't want to be one of them." I smiled. "I may need your help though. Apparently a group of vampires called Red want me."

"What?" Chase asked me. He gave me a straight face. "It's good you aren't one of them, because they lied again."

I crossed my arms, "or you lied again."

Chase put his face in his hands, "look, I said I was sorry, but I'm not lying. I know when the Red are up to something, and they aren't right now."

My eyebrows furrowed. "How, exactly?"

"My Dad is the overall leader of the vampire world, and he always asks for my help to try to kill them out." Chase bit his lip, and gave me a pointed look. "I never help, but he always asks no matter what. I mean, I don't really trust the guy."

I smirked. "I understand, since I can't trust Amara, and all the rest of my owners," I put air quotations around "owner." "Is it just me, or are you thinking that we should take those jerks out once and for all?"

Chase smiled. "Is it just me, or is this really weird?"

I burst out laughing. "Remember when I called you Sir?" We both started to laugh for five straight minutes, because of how dumb I was.

"Yeah, yeah," Chase recalled. "Just so you know, you were my first catch," Chase smiled sheepishly. "I said it so you wouldn't doubt me."

I laughed harder and punched him lightly on the shoulder. "I knew it!"

"Well you didn't notice I was lying at the time," Chase and I started our encore of laughs again. He kicked the ground softly. "I had no idea what to do," Chase looked into my eyes and grinned even wider. "I guess it worked though, since I have caught three others." His smile suddenly disappeared. "I wasn't planning to tell you that."

"Eh," I kept the smile on my face. "I don't like any other vampires, so keep at it!"

"I've seen a lot, but you are by far my favorite vampire," Chase blushed a little, but then it disappeared. "For one, you actually don't act like a droid."

"I know! It's ridiculous how they act." I sat down and leaned back on the same wall I did when Chase first kidnapped me, but this time, he didn't flinch like I was going to attack him.

"You know, I used to have a best friend," I racked my brain for actual good memories of her, seeing I haven't had any good ones with her for a while. "Her name is Riley, and she's a droid now."

Chase scoffed. "Let me guess, all vampires are known as droids to you now?"

I held a sheepish grin, "maybe."

He pretended to be disturbed and put his face in his hands. "What have I done?" He asked me through his hands, but it sounded muffled.

I laughed, but I instantly stopped the moment I heard the door have a swift knock on it. It was loud because the inside echoed, plus my vampire hearing, which is already multiplied by two. I covered my ears of the noise, and it felt a lot better.

I looked up at Chase, and tilted my head. "Who is that?" I whispered.

"I don't know!" Chase whisper shouted. He tossed a small perfume bottle over to me. "Put that on," he ordered. "And call me Sir." He joked.

"Really Chase?" I giggled a little. "Can't resist huh?"

He shook his head no.

I quickly sprayed the bottle of liquid on my skin, and let it soak it for a moment. "I hope this works," I looked at Chase. I was thinking of doing something I have never even thought of before. I pushed off of the ground with a light push, but it was quick and slick.

Chase walked under me and gave me a disgusted look. "Wow," he laughed silently. He then moved over to the door and opened it casually. "Hello?"

I clung to the ceiling tightly, and I thought it was an odd, but cool experience. Plus, I could hear Chase very loudly and clearly. I could also see who it was at the door. Obviously no threat, it was Simon! The only thing I was scared of now was he would ask me out! He was a little creep!

"Um, sure Simon, I'll be right out." Chase muttered, and slammed the door in Simon's face. "Kylie, come down now! Just not on me…"

"What was that?! You want me to land on you?" We both laughed. I liked Chase. When I was with him, all we do is laugh. With the council and Riley, all I do is hope they won't kill me.

Huh. I remember when Chase threatened to kill me. Everything was really different now. Keeping in mind I was a vampire who never sleeps, I suck human blood, and I never knew I was adopted. Let's also not forget my best friend at the moment is a vampire hunter, and I'm a vampire. Usually vampire + vampire hunter = vampire with a stake in its heart. But not with this situation!

I let myself drop from the ceiling, and landed on my feet with ease.

Chase snorted, "I can't remember when seeing that wasn't normal." He glanced up to where I clung, and scoffed a little to himself.

"I can!" I put in. "Wait…" I suddenly stopped in a questionable way. "How does Simon know where our base is?"

"Our base?" He smiled again. "That works for me."

"Me too because you're un-armed right now," I joked and kicked up my foot in a mocking gesture. "You got lucky."

"Oh, I'm always armed." He pulled a large garlic piece out of his pants pocket, and threw it at me purposely, leaving me frozen and him the upper hand.

"Ha ha!" He said like a madman.

"Seriously Chase?" I asked, still suspended in time.

Chase looked down, "it's still funny," He let me see his evil grin.

"Okay, madman, why is Simon here?" I wondered with a touch of jealously. At the moment, I wanted Chase all to myself.

Wow. Why was I acting like he was my possession? I was acting like, "If you steal him from me, I'll report you to the cops!"

"Not important, but after this wears off, I'm kicking you out! We don't want the same thing to happen as last time." Chase ran his fingers through his hair, not even once did he stop smiling.

"The one thing I remember from last time is that Simon is a total fan boy! Does he actually love me?" I asked in disgust. "I'm sorry; I bet you've gathered from that I think he's clingy."

"Eh, he kind of is."

"Some friend you are," I said sarcastically, but jokingly at the same time. "Anyways, there's one thing I still need to discuss with you." I just had a bad thought. "I think the council is targeting you."

"What?" Chase scoffed. "They don't even know I exist."

"Remember when I said they lied that Red was back? Yeah well, they said the only way to take them out is to have a VAMPIRE HUNTER take them out." I put extra enthusiasm into "vampire hunter."

Chase's face went blank as he processed the information. "You know, now that you mention it, I think they might."

"Then I guess we better be working on a plan." I looked him hard in the eyes, and he nodded.

He backed up and turned away. He opened the door smoothly, almost like I would. Well except it being very close to weightless for me. "Hey, Simon, ugh," he fake groaned. "I just tripped and hurt my knee, I can't come, sorry man." He closed the door slowly, acting like he couldn't close it any faster.

I raised an eyebrow, "what was all the, oh man," I grabbed my knee and seethed my teeth just as the garlic affect wore off. "Ooh, ow, that hurts dude."

Chase made his hand into a dismissive gesture. "I'll tell you later, but right now my main focus is not being murdered by your mom."

I put my hand on my hip, "I've never heard that one and I never thought I would."

"Okay," Chase pulled over a black chair, turned it around, and sat in it backwards so that the back was facing me.

"So I'm thinking we take the easiest ones first, so then we can save Amara for last." I sat in the same exact place as I had two times before. "Got to save the best for last, right?" I asked him, hoping that he would agree.

"Yes," he agreed.

I did a silent cheer for myself that he liked my idea, considering he was like a vampire expert, between being a vampire hunter and having his dad being the overall vampire ruler of the world.

"I say we pick off Cassidy first, since she's the least important, then Mason, Faith, and Amara. Sound good?" Chase asked me.

"Yup," I looked at him seriously. "How do we actually single them out though? They are always hanging around other people, especially Mason and Cassie." I looked up at the hard ceiling, in which I hung on to a couple minutes ago.

"Hmm…" Chase thought hard as did I.

"I could lure them out by saying, "oh my gosh! There's a human checking out the shack!" Then when they run out since it's so urgent, you'll be there, acting like an idiot, then BAM! You strike 'em and haul 'em away!" I smiled.

"YES!" Chase stood up. "I can leave them in here until we've rounded them all up!"

"Okay, now since we have the basic plan figured out, let's take our time. Because next time I land in jail, they aren't going to let me out." I pointed out while Chase nodded with my reasoning.

"Plus, if they do attack, I am always armed." Chase smirked at the garlic on the floor where he had hit me with it.

"Hey, maybe while we're at it we might as well overthrow them." I suggested.

"Yes," Chase got an evil smirk on his face. "We should wait a week, and then get Cassidy so they won't expect it."

"That's what I was thinking, but in six days, my parents are going to think that I get home that day from a trip with Riley. So I basically mean the ropes are going to be tighter on me." I admitted.

"You still snuck out when they knew you were home, so I think your fine," Chase pointed out as he sat back down.

"Yeah, I don't think that just kidnapping and overthrowing them is enough for all they have done to us though." I honestly said to Chase. It was my turn to stand up, so I did. "I just feel like they deserve more than that, are you thinking the same thing?"

"Totally," Chase snorted. "So this is what I think we should do..."

Chapter 12

I T WAS 2:00 A.M. six days later, and I had to go hunting. I also had to go home at 10:00 PM today, which was actually quite depressing. I liked having the freedom with Chase all the time, but now I won't. My parents still think I'm a perfectly normal thirteen year old girl! They would have a heart attack if they found out I was doing things this dangerous, and hurting people on purpose.

Since I've been a vampire for a while now, and I understood how things worked, I felt little remorse for what I did. Especially getting revenge on the council.

I just landed on the side of a house near the park. It was smaller than Riverside houses, but still fairly large. It was brown, with lighter brown places where the weather had hit it hard.

I looked up at the window, and pushed off the ground. In a huge burst of wind and blurriness, the next time I was visible was on the side of the house. I tore off the screen and opened the unlocked window.

I hopped in, and popped out my fangs in a quick motion. I looked over at a girl with orange wavy hair, and tons of freckles. I knew her! I mean I didn't know her name, but I've seen her around school. She was going to be a seventh grader this year.

I walked over to her door calmly, knowing how this worked. I had to dodge multiple items in the medium sized room because it was so messy.

There was a faint clicking noise when I tried locked the door. I looked at the lock closer when I had to press it multiple times to make it lock.

I looked back at her, feeling really bad. She was smart.

This girl installed her own lock. You could tell by the condition of the doorknob that people tried to get in a lot. It was badly damaged, and I could smell blood on it.

I walked back over to the girl like a mouse, because I was so quiet. I bent down and looked at her face. Scratched and bruised like I thought.

I sighed. I was pretty lucky. My adoptive Mom would never abuse me. Even Amara may be a terrible mom, but she never hurt me on purpose when she knew I was her daughter. This doesn't mean Chase and I won't get revenge, but I knew even though Amara lies a lot and she was kind of a jerk along with the rest of the council that she wouldn't intentionally beat me.

Ugh. Whatever, this would help her. At least once she was a vampire her wounds that her parents gave her would disappear.

I hissed, and that woke her up right away. I mean, she has to be forced to have good reflexes if she gets beat by her parents.

She didn't scream though, knowing her parents surely wouldn't help her. She just backed up in her little twin sized bed, and finally she just fell off.

I lunged in, and my pointy fangs dung into her pale skin, creating a blood stream down her neck, staining her pajamas with even more blood.

After she was knocked out, I stood up, and hopped onto the windowsill. I really hope she becomes a vampire. Then she can heal faster. It would be better for her.

Instead of going off and flying at an amazing speed, I decided I could walk, since I had a couple of hours until sunrise. I jumped off of the windowsill and landed on the lush grass with my feet.

I walked around the house and started to wander the neighborhood. Just in case I ran into anybody, I put my fangs away.

I thought about the plan. Today is Cassidy, tomorrow is Mason, the next day is Faith, and then we just have to get Amara when we can because she is going to be on edge. So if you think about it, it won't take very long. After we kidnap them all, we have them meet our demands!

Then I thought about going home. It will be nice to act normal for a while again.

Wait.

I haven't even thought about how they lied to me too! They always said that I was theirs! Now, I have serious proof that I am totally not theirs!

I should have guessed that I was adopted before, though. Because I've always noticed that everybody in my family had straight blonde hair, and I had wavy black hair.

Whatever, at least they didn't imprison me, so I'll let this one slide. I'm already fed up with everybody else's lies too, so what difference does it make that I'm fed up with this one now too?

I kept walking along the road, kicking small rocks lightly when I saw one. I looked around cautiously; making sure no one was there so I could take off to a club.

No one was, so I pushed off of the ground, and before I knew it, I landed at those rusty stairs that all vampire things started with.

I was about to open the trap door, but then I smelt humans. I turned around, and saw six really big kids in hoods and sweatpants looking at me.

Oh… crud.

I could so get away, but these people aren't used to seeing thirteen year old girls with freaky abnormal strength who could also fly.

"Look what the cat dragged in," one of them said with a deep voice. He was the shortest, but still a foot taller than me.

They inched closer, trying to be intimidating. It probably would have worked if I wasn't the strongest being who ever lived.

"Can I help you?" I asked standing my ground like I usually would. These boys had no idea who they were messing with, and more importantly, what they were messing with.

"Can I help you?" Another one joked mockingly.

"Fine," I sighed. "What do you want?"

The tallest walked forward and got way too close to me. He got an inch away from my face and said with a stone hard voice, "you're coming with us."

The rest of the group gathered around me, creating a circle.

Okay, these gangster people wanted to kidnap me, so surely that calls for some vampire powers, right? I mean, they couldn't even really see me. There was only a dim streetlight that was a couple yards away giving them light, but me, I could see them perfectly.

"I wouldn't do that if I were you," I threatened them. I showed no fear, because they weren't scary! They were kind of creepy though. Like Faith's smiles!

They all started to laugh so hard, it made me want to laugh at them. After I finished them, they weren't going to be laughing.

I pushed off of the mushy ground softly, and landed outside of the circle in a millisecond.

I gave them an innocent smile. "Like I was saying?" I crossed my arms and stared them down.

"How did you do that?" A new speaker wondered while they all stared at the thirteen year old girl in utter awe.

I pushed off of the ground again, and landed on the other side of them, by the trap door. I smirked. "Boo!" I yelled suddenly.

They all screamed and ran away, into the woods.

Being in those woods at night meant you aren't coming out for a while! I bet they would rather deal with me instead of the council. Still, I couldn't help laughing at the group of boys. They just got scared by a thirteen year old girl!

I opened the trap door all the way this time, and ran down the stairs. The music was loud like last time, and it had about twenty vampires too.

I sat down in a booth and sat there for a while, just admiring my surroundings. It was so cool! I mean, most of the vampires were wearing black everything, but others were wearing something as light as white! That goes for the objects in the club as well, and that made me happy.

It's kind of nice to know it's not weird that I'm the only vampire wearing a light blue crop top. I mean, I also was wearing these cool metallic black shorts too, but that was my honest choice, not the vampire in me choosing.

I bolted upright as I saw a counter in the far right corner. I didn't know what it was, so I decided I would go figure that out.

There was a vampire behind the counter, texting someone. She looked up as she saw me.

The girl had blonde hair, dark red lipstick, a gray and red striped shirt, brown eyes, and I couldn't see her pants because the counter was so high.

"Sup," the girl greeted me. "Want a chain?" She ducked below the counter and came back up with a black chain.

"Um, sure, how much does it cost?" I wondered.

"Nothing," she simply said. She handed me the chain, and pulled her phone back out and instantly began to text again.

"Thanks," I mumbled as I attached the chain to a belt hoop. I looked down at it after I placed it right, and decided it was pretty cool. I walked away.

I sat back in the same booth, and closed my eyes for a couple of minutes to relax because I felt kind of stressed. Once I opened them again I felt a lot better for an odd reason. The stress was gone, and for the first time in a week, I was happy to go home.

I walked into the entryway of my house, and was greeted by my parents.

"Kylie!" Mom exclaimed as she enveloped me in a hug. "I noticed you forgot your stuff. Did Riley let you borrow some of her items?"

I nodded yes as she let me go. "Yeah, it was really nice of her..." I tried to lie convincingly. I can't believe that I just said Riley did something nice. Those two words should never go into a sentence together, ever.

"Oh, we never got the chance to tell you that the Anderson's are here to visit today," Dad jerked his thumb towards the kitchen behind him.

The Andersons are family friends. They have a daughter my age, named Karly. She has long straight blonde hair, and kind of a bad attitude. Not around adults though. Around adults she's a little angel. When she is around me and other kids, she's a big devil alright.

Last time she was here, I was blackmailed into giving her a two hour back massage so she wouldn't lie to my parents about me breaking one of their nice vases.

If it comes down to them having to believe one of us, it would end up being Karly.

Of course Karly and Ari are friends though. Both brats!

I forced a smile to my parents. "Great," I said through gritted teeth. "So, just out of curiosity, when do they leave?" I looked away and put in a small frown, like I would be sad if they left. "Hopefully it's not soon," I sighed like I really liked them.

"Oh, I'm sorry honey. They have to leave right after dinner," Mom came over and started to rub my arm in a sympathetic gesture.

Man! Couldn't they leave sooner? Then never come back?

"Well, I'm going to go see my friend, bye now!" I spun around to run out of the door as fast as a human possibly could. When I talk about Chase now, I call him a friend because my parents would never approve of me seeing this boy too much.

"Only if you bring Karly with you," Dad abruptly stated. "If you want to see your friend, I'm sure Karly will like her too."

You've got to be kidding me! I hated Karly more than Riley, and that's a pretty good accomplishment on Karly's part.

I kept my cool. "Okay," I told him calmly. "Hey Karly want to come to the park with me?!" I yelled, desperately hoping the answer was no.

Karly walked out of the kitchen and into the hallway. "Aw, sorry Ky," she began.

KY!? She has no right to give me a nickname!

I don't call her Kar, because I really don't want to. If I gave her a nickname, it would be like we were actually friends...

"I would love to, but the little one wants me stay," She looked back at Ari who just walked out of the kitchen.

"Aw, that's a shame," I said with fake emotion. "Bye now!" I opened the door, and it squealed with its usual creakiness. I ran out into fresh air and took a gigantic breath.

Thank goodness she said no! Now I can get to our base in a minute, and we can discuss our revenge plan. We already had it figured out; we just need to make sure Chase has his props.

I checked around me for nearby people, and found nobody was there. I ran as fast as I could behind a big bushy tree, and pushed off of the ground as hard as I could.

I zoomed through the sky with speeds of a rocket, and arrived at Chase's base in mere minutes, when it would usually take about an hour.

Now that I was actually cool with being a vampire, there were some serious advantages to it. I could run faster than a car!

I opened the door, knowing he would be here, since he always is. When I opened the vampire proof door, I got greeted by two people, instead of a lone Chase.

Chase was sitting in a chair, pointing one of his garlic guns at a vampire. Her face was down, and her golden blonde hair was really messy.

Chase's stare faded on the girl once he saw me. He smirked and bit his lip at the same time, making a fake guilty emotion.

"Sorry, I got the chance, so I went in for the kill," he pointed at the girl. "So tonight, we're doing Mason," Chase stood up.

What was he talking about?

I walked over to the girl, and bent over. I took the hair out of her face to be greeted by an unhappy vampire giving me the, "once I'm out of here you're dead" look.

I backed up, smiling. "Nice job Chase," I patted Chase on the back. "Cassidy is down, so all we have left is Mason, Faith, and Amara." I crossed my arms and looked at Cassidy with an evil smile. Maybe now she will regret being a total power freak!

"Last night I saw her, so I just took one down," Chase sat back down. "Now I'm babysitting her just in case she has any intentions of escape." He looked over at me. "It's kind of fun, actually. It's going to be hilarious seeing them all power- deprived."

I laughed at that, "that is another pleasure coming out of it."

"Oh shut up Kylie!" Cassidy shrieked at me. "Once I'm out of here, the rest of the council and I are going to throw you back into the jail!" She paused for a moment, so you could tell she just had a better idea. "No, instead we would probably make you a servant 24/7!" She laughed. "We'll see who's laughing then."

"Probably still me, 'cause who said anything about ever letting you go?" I had to try to act serious, because when I said that I was trying to give her a heart attack. "By the way," I added casually, "you do realize when you said that you were laughing."

Chase scoffed. "If you two ladies are done chatting, I'd like to say something." He raised his eyebrows at me in particular.

I kind of glanced back him. "You think I'm a lady?"

"Judging by that weird chain, no," he laughed at me.

I flipped my hair, "it's a new fashion sense," I stuck my tongue out at him. He chuckled to himself softly. "Okay, I bought it this morning because I was bored and it was free."

"That's what-"

Cassidy cut him off.

"Okay, what were you going to say?!" Cassidy asked Chase very loudly.

Chase didn't look at Cassidy, but listened to her. "So remember how to get Mason?" He wondered aloud, not giving any information about our kidnapping plan away to Cassidy.

I nodded solemnly. I pointed my gaze towards Cassidy. "Now let's have some fun."

Chapter 13

I ARRIVED AT MY house at about 7:00p.m., and apparently everybody was waiting for me to come back for dinner so we could all eat together.

Although I could technically eat them for dinner, but anyways, I was in a bad position because they were having my favorite meal... chicken alfredo.

It would usually bring me lots of pleasure besides the fact that it has garlic in it, and it's not very normal that suddenly a teenager just freezes up and can't move because of garlic.

Except it's not weird for me anymore, and that's kind of weird.

I sat down, and everybody started to dig in... leaving me in an awkward place because I was just sitting there with a fake smile on my face.

"Honey, it's your favorite meal, why aren't you having any?" Mom asked right before she piled a forkful of chicken alfredo into her mouth.

It's bad enough I would to need to eat it, but the smell was terrible!

I shrugged and took the big spoon, putting a little chicken alfredo on my plate and trying to think of a way to avoid eating it at once.

It's too bad when you become a vampire you don't get super-smarts, because that would come in very handy right about now.

I was just staring at the noodles and chicken while my family and our guests stared at me.

I gave them all a halfhearted smile that never even came close to reaching my eyes. "You know, I'm not really hungry," I lied in a soft voice that had mixed emotions in it.

"Kylie, you're thirteen," Mom gave me a strict straight forward face. "You should eat your dinner; you're not a toddler anymore!" Mom stared me down angrily. "Why won't you eat your favorite meal?"

"Yeah, Kylie," Karly put in, only making my situation worse. "You aren't a toddler anymore. I'm younger than you and I'm eating it," Karly put a forkful of food in her mouth.

It took all my strength and not to hop on the table and scream at Karly. This was one of her "angel ways" to everybody else. Only I could tell that she was making fun of me in her head, and later it was going to be out loud.

The pressure I got from everybody made me pick up my fork, and I slowly brought it to my mouth. I suddenly dropped it, making a clinking noise on the plate.

"Oh," I groaned and grabbed my stomach. "My stomach hurts so bad..." I lied, and stood up. "I better go lay down in bed..." I ran off before anybody could say anything, so I wouldn't be forced to eat garlic, or stay in the room with Karly anymore.

I shut the door behind me, and almost wanted to collapse into bed like I said. I wasn't exhausted, but I was getting butterflies about tonight.

I knew Mason liked to street hunt, so Chase was going to pretend to be some dork in a track suit walking along the dark streets.

I sighed as I smelt someone coming. Karly.

She opened the door. "Hey loser, why are you being so lame?" Karly crossed her arms, expecting an answer as if she were a princess.

Could I bite her? I looked outside. Nope. Man, why couldn't it be dark out?!

"My stomach hurts," I grabbed it. "Now leave me alone before you regret it." I waved her off right before I had a super bad urge to pop my fangs and kill her.

She left quickly, as she must have sensed I would actually do something dangerous. Good for her, she must be catching on!

Whoa.

I got to slow down. Well, it's definitely showing I'm a vampire, because I've never thought that way in my life before. I'm not a psycho killer, but I'm getting there!

I groaned and sat down. Now to wait until 11:00p.m., when I get to kidnap Mason! It sounded bad, but it was good because he wasn't a good person. Or vampire, in this lifestyle.

Whatever, it still excited me, especially since I got to see Chase in a dorky outfit. Believe me, after we succeed, I was never going to let him live that down. Never is a long time, when you're a vampire that is.

I was still just excited about the whole thing. I mean, after what they all did to me, I would get revenge, and who doesn't want that?

I sat down on my bed and popped my fangs out. I didn't want to spend the next four hours pretending to be sick. I looked over at the window.

I walked over to it and just stared out of it for a moment. I looked downwards and saw the place on the side of the house that I hit when I couldn't control my speed.

I chuckled to myself a little. I was still myself, just a little vampire added. I can't deny that since I can run up to 400 miles per hour. Okay, maybe more than a little vampire, but the point is I'm still myself.

I opened my window and jumped on the windowsill, so I was crouched down. I dived out of the window headfirst and landed on my feet perfectly with a soft thud. I checked around to make sure no one was watching me, so I just pushed off the ground really hard and went soaring through the air.

I was used to the wind now, and the speed. I thought I'd have a little fun quickly.

I landed right outside of Faith's shack and had an odd sensation in my mind on how to have that fun. I was just going to even the playing field with Chase.

I walked in the shack, and down the forbidding stairs. I acted calm when I reached the bottom, even though I was freaking out. I really shouldn't be doing this. It was too risky.

But too tempting!

There was a human slave walking past me with a laundry basket in hand. I put my hand out in front of her to make her stop.

"Hey, do you know where Faith is right now?" I asked the girl politely. I kind of felt bad for her though, because she is stuck here permanently, and I was going to be forced to do that if I wasn't so stubborn. And plus this girl only looked a year younger than me, and that's too young to start working for the rest of your life.

Or how ever long they keep these people working here, because I didn't know for sure. I hope it isn't for life for the girl's sake.

"She's out taking care of some business at the park." The girl said solemnly, not having the courage to look me in the eyes because all she would see is death and destruction. I kind of wanted to see her eyes though, because they were a pretty hazel color and she had dark brown hair.

"What's keeping you here?" I blurted out suddenly, wondering why she doesn't bolt when she's not being watched.

The girl's head sprung upwards towards me as I asked the question. She gently set down the laundry basket and pointed at an electronic ankle bracelet.

My eyes grew soft and my mouth dropped. "Oh..."

That's a little harsh, even for the council.

"Does that disappoint you?" The girl hurriedly asked. "I can make it up to you!"

I looked at her seriously. "The only thing you need to make up is your life." I turned around and ran out as fast as I could to the park.

In my mind it just clicked that Chase's base in over there, and Faith had to "take care of some business," by business did she mean Chase?

Moments later I arrived at the park to see my fears were true. Chase was standing in the middle of the park with his hands on his head with his elbows out, meaning he was surrendering. Why was he surrendering?! Didn't he keep garlic on him at all times?

He keeps garlic that he can throw, but Faith wasn't playing around. There was almost no way he would be able to hit her when she was running.

I hid behind a tree, remembering that I still had that special spray thing on so other vampires couldn't smell me.

I tried to slow down my breathing so she couldn't hear me, and it worked! I listened in on what they were saying. I couldn't see them behind the tree.

"So you're the vampire hunter that's disrupting us?" Faith asked in a stone hard voice, much like the ones I've heard before.

I could hear Faith super speed over, and I almost freaked out. She was not going to lay a finger on him, if she does; she's going to regret it.

"Kylie…" Chase whispered uncomfortably.

"What's that?" Faith chuckled.

Even though I couldn't see Faith, I knew she pulled out one of her creepy smiles on Chase. I didn't want him to bear that. I couldn't even bear it.

In a slick and too fast motion, I ran out from behind the tree and tackled Faith to the ground. Since I was stronger, I pinned her to the ground.

"Now!" I yelled.

Chase pulled the garlic out of his pocket, sprinted over to where I was awkwardly restraining Faith, and shoved it in her shoe.

I picked up Faith and put her on my shoulder. I turned to Chase. "Meet you at the base." I ran with Faith into the base and laid her down where Cassidy was sitting with garlic on her.

I stood before them, with the biggest smile plastered on my face. "Don't worry, Mason will be joining you soon." All of the sudden, I felt my chest. I wasn't breathing.

Both girls laughed at me as they noticed what I just realized. "Didn't you know that you could stop breathing? It's a part of being immortal. Most vampires only breathe when they are around humans," Faith told me.

"Shut up, we both know that I can do whatever I want to do to you right now," I pointed out as Chase walked in the door.

"So Kylie, I was thinking that we get Mason and Amara tonight, because I guess we're on a roll," he looked over to Cassidy and Faith.

I smirked. "I think I could deal with that. It's getting dark, so you better go dress up." Chase walked over to the corner with a Justin Bieber wig and aviators.

He slipped on the aviators. "How do I look?"

He looked really cute in them! Okay, maybe more than cute. Hot.

I smiled dimly. "Okay." I wanted to tell him how I actually felt, but it would never work. I'm a vampire, and he's a vampire hunter.

"Only okay?" He joked, but a part of me felt like he wasn't joking. Almost like he wanted me to tell him I liked him.

It was 11:00p.m., and Chase was roaming the dim streets really stupidly, by adding his own little walk to his Justin Bieber and aviator glasses era. Let me just tell you that you would not want to see that! He looked like a drunken bear who had wandered into a neighborhood in the city. I was surprised he hasn't hit a tree by now.

I had rubbed myself in that weird spray again, so Mason couldn't detect my presence that easily considering I was also wearing Chase's black cloak. When he first hunted me, I couldn't detect his features, so I don't think that Mason will find it easy to find mine.

Anyways, Chase was still loitering the street, trying to desperately stay in character because he could tell I was silently making fun of him. I couldn't blame him though. If it was the other way around, I would be about to break character and Chase would be making fun of me!

I had to stifle my laughs when Chase actually tripped, and fell flat on his face. And on his Justin Bieber wig! When he got back up he brushed off his shoulders and continued to be a drunken bear. Except this time the drunken bear ran into a tree because when he fell he broke his aviators.

I put my face in my hands to stop myself from erupting into an explosion of laughs.

I stopped laughing after I heard a vampire land on the cement. I instantly shot my head up to look at Chase behind the tree with my vampire reflexes.

Of course it was Mason, who was smiling evilly with his fangs and red eyes right at Chase. Mason was wearing light brown shorts and a black T-shirt, laughing at chase who was wearing broken aviators, a Justin Bieber wig, and an eighties track suit. "What happened to you, time warp?" Mason asked as he circled Chase creepily, ready to strike, but was too interested with Chase's looks right now.

"Really dude? That's not very..." Chase trailed off, trying to say something stupid to distract him even more. "Rad, man," he finished after he thought about it for a moment. "Like, man, did you go through a time warp too? I mean you just went," He put up his hands and quickly put them down gesturing him landing after he flew, "whoosh."

I rated his score on how stupid he was being, and right now he had an eight. Maybe he can make it a nine if he keeps going at it!

"No," Mason stated, realizing that dissing wouldn't work with this, seeing Chase's best zinger was really poorly structured like he planned. "Don't you notice the fangs, red eyes, and me flying?"

"Uh..." Chase stroked his chin pretending to think about it. He stopped stroking his chin and got really close to Mason's face examining his eyes and teeth hard. "Nope, I don't see anything."

Mason threw his arms up in the air in defeat.

See, Chase just earned a nine, seeing he was stupid for getting that close to Mason's face. If I was human still, I wouldn't want to do that. He also earned a half point for adding the extra pizazz.

Chase just started to do a really dumb laugh, which you could tell annoyed Mason a lot by the look on his face.

When the vampire food annoys the vampire, the vampire is going to attack soon, so that was my cue to come in.

I flew up in the air, landed right behind Mason, and grabbed his arms before he could react. I held them very tightly behind him and stood my ground so he wouldn't fly away. In the process my hood fell down. I couldn't see his face, but I could tell he saw my face and was annoyed that a thirteen year old girl was stronger than him and that I had just outsmarted him. I mean, I would be angry too, who wouldn't seeing he's a sixteen year old boy?

Chase sprinted over to a faraway bush down a block as fast as he could, and came back a minute later, and did the ritual of shoving the garlic down their shoes so they couldn't move.

"Hmm, maybe you should've followed your instincts about the nearby garlic. Even though it was a block away, it could still paralyze you." I told Mason, making him only feel worse about the whole situation. We purposely put it down a block because vampires could detect faraway smells, and how far away they were, not exactly, but in a range.

So Mason knew it was there, he just didn't think it would matter.

Big mistake.

I shifted Mason to the left of me so I could see dorky Chase clearly. "So I'll go drop him off with Faith and Cassidy-"

"You're the ones who captured them too?!" Mason interrupted me angrily. I knew he wanted to at least struggle to escape, but we were even depriving him of that.

"Then meet you at Faith's shack to find Amara? Or should I say soon to be our shack?" I smiled at Chase, and he smiled back.

We both knew I would arrive first, but this neighborhood was really close to Clutch woods, and of course Chase knew where the shack was if we were to overthrow them!

I pushed off the ground and entered the air in milliseconds. I could tell Mason was amazed by the speed I was going since I could practically go twice as fast as him. I also knew that he was also feeling the pain of the wind shear since he is less powerful then a human right now.

Minutes later I landed on the plump grass in front of Chase's base and opened the door with almost no effort and pushed Mason right next to Cassidy and Faith who were surprised that Chase and I caught him.

Words weren't a factor anymore.

They all knew Amara was next, and there was no denying it.

Especially when you're me, the strongest vampire who has ever lived. Watch out Amara, because you're next.

Chapter 14

I STRUTTED INTO THE shack, looking for a maid to ask where the whereabouts of Amara were. I finally found a vampire maid who came to me after she saw I was waiting.

She looked fifteen, with dark eyeliner, and all black clothing. At the moment, you wonder why she is even alive. Well she already is dead technically, but anyways I mean dead, dead. She looks like she has nothing to live for. That's either the council's fault, or hers. In my case, I'm guessing the council's fault.

"Where is Amara?" I asked the girl politely as she stared at me with her dead eyes and her dead look.

"In that empty room down the hall, Room 45," the girl answered with an I-don't-care-at-all voice. The part that freaked me out the most about her was her nose piercing.

I don't know, maybe it was her fault! Maybe she was Goth before she was even a vampire. We all know how those types of people are, so maybe it wasn't the council's fault.

It didn't matter. Revenge is revenge. And revenge shows no mercy.

"Well, do you know when she is going to leave the shack next?" I wondered hoping it was soon, and because I didn't really want to talk to this girl.

"Not for a really long time," she said with the same voice. "She's on total lockdown because Cassidy and Faith have been kidnapped."

I rolled my eyes. Great.

I didn't bother with "thanks" because I knew it wouldn't matter to the girl. Instead, I just zoomed right out of the shack to Chase where he was waiting.

"We have to go in," I closed my eyes. Going in was a bad thing seeing there were so many people in that little shack!

Chase nodded and walked in.

I followed him and grabbed his wrist and started to run super-fast to Room 45. We couldn't risk walking in with garlic and a human. After I got there, I shut the door in relief to see Amara alone. She wasn't surprised to see me come in with Chase, though.

"I've been expecting you to come for me," Amara said solemnly without turning to face Chase and me. She was just staring at the blank black wall.

It was kind of like one of those horror movies with the villain with their back towards you, and they are petting a cat. Except Amara wasn't petting a cat.

"So are you saying you're surrendering?" I asked hopefully, even though it was obviously a stupid question. "We both know that I'm more powerful than you, especially with Chase."

"I wouldn't be too sure about that." She turned around, and suddenly ten vampire guards ran in. Two grabbed Chase and his garlic gun, and the rest restricted me. I may have been really strong, but not strong enough to take out eight vampire guards.

I groaned. "You okay Chase?"

"Yup," he answered quietly, but it was pretty loud to everybody else in the room.

"What do you want, Amara?" I asked with a serious tone in my voice and on my face. "I don't care if you do force me to do my time in your petty vampire jail, and I'll be your maid for a year. Wait, not for a year. I don't want to spend too much time with the creepy Gothic vampire girl." I sighed, "Just do not hurt Chase." The last sentence I said loudly, and intimidatingly.

Amara crossed her arms and sighed.

"Let's not forget how you guys made those poor people be your maids," I struggled to break free at that time. "Even that's a little over the top for you, Amara. The girl had an ankle bracelet."

"That wasn't our fault," Amara rolled her eyes. "She was imprisoned by Red, and they put the ankle bracelet on her, and we couldn't get it off. It shocks her if she gets too far off the premises, so she's stuck here for now. She chooses to work even if we tell her she doesn't need to. And about the Gothic vampire servant, she committed a crime. She tried to kill Mason. Plus she was already creepy before we got her." Amara explained exasperatedly.

Well that makes the council seem a little, better, but not great.

"Wow, what a surprise," I told Amara sarcastically. "Is that what's going to happen to me now?" I wondered with a touch of sadness.

"As tempting as that all sounds, I'm not doing that to you, even though I do want you to accept a few terms of mine," Amara told me while walking closer. "You'll stop hurting, kidnapping, and stealing items from the vampire council."

"Fine," I rolled my eyes. "Then you stop hunting Chase and you don't force me to be on the dumb vampire council." I tried to negotiate with her. If Amara was going to get her way, I wanted a little bit of my way too!

"Okay and you also need to be with me more often. I'm still your mom, and I want to catch up with you on the past thirteen years we lost. If you agree, I promise, no more lies." Amara offered. She stood in front of me, giving me the new guidelines.

"Yes, Ma'am," I looked down at the floor. I can't believe we failed! I guess it wasn't all bad seeing Amara did feel bad what she'd done to me, but still!

"And Kylie?" I looked up at Amara. "Knock it off with Sir and Ma'am." Amara turned to Chase. "I expect you to not do it either, since we are going to have to chat if a boy is spending that much time with my daughter," Amara smiled at both of us.

"Amara!" I whined. "You're embarrassing me!" It was only about three minutes and we were already acting the typical mother daughter pair. Maybe I can tolerate Amara and the rest of the council.

Chase laughed out loud, and Amara dismissed the guards with a wave of the hand.

"Now come give me a hug," She held out her arms.

"Don't push it," I glared at her. "It's going to take time, okay?" I crossed my arms. "Can you leave for a couple minutes please? I need to talk to Chase."

Chase's face went blank as I said that.

Amara left in a second, after she expanded her grin wider knowing she had just gained her daughter back for real this time.

Although she forgot to close the soundproof doors, I laughed and ran over and closed and locked it quickly and then returned to my original place.

Was she going to try to listen in on our conversation?

I had to chuckle at the thought of it.

"Listen Chase, I need to talk to you because I have to admit something." I started off, hoping I wasn't going too fast. "We've seemed to have gotten to know each other really well over the past couple weeks and..."

Chase chuckled nervously.

"I like you," I smiled after I finally pushed it out.

My heart broke when he told me the unsettling news right after I poured my feelings out to him, and this made me regret it.

He started to laugh. "I like you too, but we both already knew that, we're friends. That was a joke, wasn't it? Acting really emotional on purpose to get laughs, right? I mean the thought of you and I is stupid, isn't it?" Chase laughed more as I forced a grin and laughed uneasily.

"Yup, it's a joke," I looked down. "Well, we better go," I said changing the topic before he realized I meant it. "We should go release Faith, Cassidy, and Mason." By we, I meant me. He couldn't see me when I was depressed over "a joke."

I ran out of the room as fast as I could to go release the council, so then I would have the base alone for a while.

Until the heart breaker shows. And maybe he will strike again. Who knows anymore, guys are so unpredictable.

A month later my relationship with Amara advanced a lot, and I was even visiting the shack daily now. The only thing she told me to do is make sure I don't use my full powers anymore. I still can, but she has been teaching me only go halfway because she tells me that there are some people who could take advantage of me. How can they though if they don't know who I am?

Chase was still my only friend, and we still hung out together a lot. I still haven't forgotten how he thought he and I were bad together, but I still tried to forget, and tried to stop trying for him. Anyways, he was now allowed into the shack and everybody was nice to him on the council.

Speaking of the rest of the council, they were now kind of nice to me and let me call them by their first names.

Right now I was carrying a basket of laundry to Faith's room because Amara told me I might be the strongest vampire ever, but I shouldn't expect special treatment, so every Wednesday and Saturday I wash and fold the laundry.

The last load I should have thrown some of my clothes in, because all of my clothes were dirty. I was wearing a stained blue blouse and really dirty sweatpants. At least I put on some of Chase's spray so vampires wouldn't annoy me about my stench.

I was walking past the entrance, when a twenty year old vampire male stopped me with his harsh words.

"Hey maid, where's Amara right now?" The guy asked. He wore dark jeans, and a red T-shirt. His features were chiseled, and he had whiskers.

"Why?" I wondered, "And by the way I'm not a maid."

"Look human," The man ran over to me and threw a fist at my face with all his strength, but I caught it obviously.

"And I'm not human."

He looked me in the eyes, "Big mistake, kid."

"Oh really?" I asked. I put down the laundry basket with the one hand I was carrying it with. "Give me a reason why?"

"I'm the new vampire ruler," The man brushed past me and kept walking on.